MW00908347

Books by Judianne Lee

Roxie's Angels

Buttercup Meadows

Laughing Lexie

Riendo Lexie

Fire, Friend or Foe

Fire Safety with Firefighter Willie

Hot

Flash

BFFs

by

Judianne

Lee

LIBRARY of CONGRESS

TXu 1-708-421

Formerly Titled: ALL NIGHTER

© Judianne Lee, 2010

ISBN 978-1-257-09913-9   Hardcover w/Sleeve

ISBN 978-0-557-97853-3   Hardcover

ISBN 978-0-557-83899-8   Soft cover

Publisher:

LULU ENTERPRISES, INC.

3101 Hillsborough Street

Raleigh, North Carolina

27607

919-459-5858

Books may be ordered from:

Odie3366@gmail.com

Lulu.com

Amazon.com

6:30 PM

Damn! Why was somebody calling me this early, when it wasn't even light yet? Momentarily disoriented, I grabbed for the offending piece of plastic, trying to end the insistent shrilling and I managed to knock it onto the floor. I gotta get a better ring on that thing, I thought as I fished it out from under the bed where it had skittered, and shoved the guilty, cold, plastic culprit to my ear.

"This better be life or death! It's six-thirty in the morning!" I growled into the phone. Sitting up, trying to sound as if I were wide awake, I tried to make my thickened voice sound alert. "Hello! Hello!" Nothing, I croaked out another, "Hello!" Now I am really pissed.

More silence. Somebody calls me and wakes me up and all I get is silence? I grabbed my much needed specs and pulled the phone away to read the ID.

Lex.

"Lex, what's the matter?" She never calls this early.

Lex said almost inaudibly, "Glory, What does an anxiety attack feel like? And by the way, it is not six-thirty in the morning. It is six-thirty in the evening. It's PM. Not AM. What's with you? And stop yelling at me."

"Oh, crap, I was so tired, I came straight home after school, fell on the bed and I really zonked out. I was up all last night reading those really earth shattering *Author Papers*. No sleep at our age will do it to me every time. By the way, why do I do this?"

"I don't know, why do you? Why isn't your TA reading them?" Lex was still speaking so quietly I was straining to hear her.

"First, you know Miranda is useless. She wants to give everybody an A. God forbid somebody might not like her. Or get their fragile feelings hurt. Every time she works on papers she feels compelled to explain every mark she makes. She even wrote some post-it-note-apologies on some of the papers I had graded. We had an interesting little discussion about that!"

"But second, and what is vastly more important, back to your question, *anxiety attack*? What's with you?" I continued, "You are the rock, Honey Bun, you are the glue in our little group. And as my BFF, you are the calm, steady one. Don't go all mushy on me. Leave that to Regina, the drama queen. For real, what's the problem?"

"I don't know, I came home, started working on my own pile of rehashed *Shakespeare* and suddenly, I just couldn't breathe, I'm still in a cold sweat and I even think I'm a little dizzy."

"OK, my little birthday friend, does this have anything to do with the looming forty-nine tomorrow? Remember the group is here for the big festivities. Happy hour or should I say happy hours? Tell Mama, *Waaats* up?" trying to do my best Budweiser silly voice. Didn't seem to be working.

"I don't know. It started in my last class today. One of the students was asking a question and I just completely zoned out. I had nothing. I had to refocus me for a change. It just got progressively worse all day. And yeah, I think it does have to do with being forty-nine," Lex answered all in a rush.

"My wee learners were doing *The Play Debates* and right in the middle, I got this flash: I have one year and then I am at the half century mark! Then I got this really stupid thought. Shakespeare died at fifty. Well, fiftyish if you want to split hairs. Is that the stupidest thing anybody could think about? Who thinks about Shakespeare dying at fifty-two and then gets a panic attack? I thought about just driving my self over to Rockland State, grabbing a little white coat and turning myself in. So much for being the calm part of our duo. Glory, its your turn to be the All-Wise-Wizard. I got nothin'. Come out from behind the curtain and help me get home to Kansas. What great piece of wisdom do you have for me?"

"Seriously, Lex, are you still having a problem? Don't want you having a heart attack. I would never survive the faculty meetings without you, My Sweet Little Buffer, who keeps me from speaking my mind. Without you the villagers would be storming my house."

"No, I feel better just talking to you. Maybe you should switch to the Psychology Department," Lex managed to joke.

I was very relived to hear her voice beginning sound a little more like herself. Lex was really scaring me; I've never heard her so unsure of herself.

"O.K., Professor BFF, I have just had one of my totally brilliant flashes. Forget my grading and yours, I can't look at another *James Joyce is just the best Author Ever* paper. I am calling out the troops. Lex, let's do "The Do" tonight instead of tomorrow." I told her as I began untangling my self from covers and a mound of my much-needed pillows.

"JJ and Reg had said that tonight was a good night for them anyway. I'll call the gang. And by the way, I know that you grade most of your papers too.   Why don't you just let Benny grade? You are loaded up with work right now, with the new book and everything."

"Same, only different," she sighed, "he is too hard on everybody who does not measure up to his self imposed standards. Why do these TAs look so good on paper and turn out to be such little shits?"

"I don't know. I don't even know why we call them Teacher Assistants. This year, not so much assisting. Every year it gets worse.   Sometimes I feel like all I do is trying to get them up to speed and then they move on," I sighed.

"When was the last time we both had good ones? I'm not even sure what a good one is." and she sighed back at me.

I really had no answer to that one, but I was glad that she was beginning to sound more like herself, and better yet, she was not objecting to changing the birthday bash night.

"All-righty then, I am hanging up and calling the Brainiacs.   By the way, who came up with that stupid name? Never mind it'll come to me. Anyway, be here by eight," I told her.

Lex hung up and I clicked a new dial tone to call Mora, told her there was a change in plans and why, then asked if she would call the others in our merry little band of higher educators.

Hanging up, I suddenly realized I had just over an hour to get things up to par for the invasion of the BFFs. Thank goodness, I am a half-way decent keeper of my abode. The clutter was almost at an acceptable level. I had enough time at least, to make it a little more presentable.   I knew I would be able to knock out what I needed to do to get ready for the group, which was mainly making sure that there would be enough food for what most likely would be a long night. Most of our celebrations had a way of becoming marathons.

I started with what I do best. I called The Canton Wok, told Chen-Chi that I wanted the usual for six people, please have Hai deliver about 8:30 and got off. Three minutes flat! Being quite pleased with my amazing hostess abilities, I turned my attention to polishing up my digs.

The bed had been perfectly made when I left for my morning classes and since I had just plopped down on top for my little unplanned snooze, all it needed was some smoothing the bed back into a somewhat presentable shape. I removed the lump under the covers that morphed into my aged pal, Hamlet. How he can get under the covers in a tightly well made bed, I do not know. In another life, he had been alternately a stud as well as quite the skunk and cat killer. I go hush-hush on the cat killer part. Makes for very nervous neighbors. I have noticed a dearth of cats in our neighborhood and I sincerely hope that it is not attributable to my little badger-avenging dog. He takes his neighborhood duties quite seriously.

Hamlet is a long-haired dachshund who has become pretty much a basketball with hair. We cuddled for a minute before I unceremoniously shoved him out of his little door that opened to his little fenced off domain to do whatever he could do poopwise. He cooperates by not leaving presents all over the larger yard that slopes down from the back decking to the sea wall which borders the mighty Hudson River. My little piece of paradise.

"Wow! Hamlet, another pound and you are going to need a bigger door. I know how you feel, Pal, sometimes I think I need a bigger door too."

I enjoyed a minute to watch him ramble around his little yard area, then nose open the gate to the larger yard and he ran down the hill with complete abandon. The river glistened, sparked and shot shards of light back at me while I reflected on Henry Hudson's words about this mighty river. "Were so pleasant with grass and flowers-and goodly trees-as ever we had seen." And it has not changed since time began if you do not count the pollution and the proliferation of houses along the bank. But I try not to think about that part. Just enjoy it for what it is. And oddly the river is one of the things that keeps me very humble and understanding my miniscule part of the cosmos.

I left Hamlet to his morning ritual of nose-to-the-ground sniffing along the long, cold trail of what ever critter has had the audacity to walk upon his hallowed grounds. Knowing I did not have time to go rambling with him, I reluctantly went back inside. The French doors that lead out onto my deck have his little door built in so he flits in and out all day long without my having to play door-woman for him.

I eyed the mild mess in my bathroom and gave it a very cursory clean up in what I determined to be an effective solution to the mess inside. It wasn't a terrible d, I just didn't want to share this lapse in my normal clean-freakiness. I would love to just close the door and do it later, but I knew that wouldn't work because with six of us, we would need all three bathrooms. So a quick once over got it to presentable.

I get teased all the time that I am obsessively anal. I guess that I am the type who gets focused on one thing and everything else goes to Hell in a hand basket. If I am working on school work or a book, the house takes the hit. Then all the sudden I can't stand the mess any more and I am cleaning from dawn to dusk. A friend told me one time that I would be a psychiatrist's delight if I would just submit to analysis. Frankly that scares the crap out of me. I think I function just fine. My luck, somebody would tell me that I need to spend thousands of dollars to find out what I already know. I'm an amalgam of my baggage. We all are. Some people learn to cope better than others. I am really tied of people who whine about their background as an excuse to treat other people badly. Oh, as usual my head is spinning in a thousand different directions. So, sue me, I am a bundle of contradictions.   Got to focus on getting ready for the group to come eat, drink and be merry.

Thank goodness for my other two bathrooms. One in the guest room and one off the living room. Spotless.   See, anal pays off.

I headed out to the living room to see where my efforts were needed. Not too bad, I observed. I started picking up the scattered student papers and started plopping them into my *unfinished basket.*

Sadly there are twice as many papers in it as there were ensconced in the *done basket.* I had bought the baskets on my last trip with the group to Aruba. The two baskets were supposed to hold something interesting and decorative. But somehow the shape and size had just screamed *papers.* Hustling the baskets to my office-study-library, I shut that door knowing all to well that somebody would need something out of it. Mora has been known to come in to make long phone calls to the boyfriend. We all wonder what she is saying every time she does this.

I glanced around my little, secluded, haven of my own making and   I thought I had done what I could for now. Scarlet said it best, there is always tomorrow.

The kitchen was already shinny clean. Chalk that up to two of my personality traits. The aforementioned anal behavior and the fact that I never cook. Works for me. I have spiffed up and ordered dinner. I am the perfect hostess! Well, at least in my head I am.

It occurred to me that there was a good chance I had been drooling and sweating during my nap. I quickly shucked my wrinkled school clothes. I grabbed a quick shower, towel dried my efficiently short, blonde hair, slapped on lip-stick, donned grey, silk slacks and my new, peach, silk cashmere sweater and judged myself presentable.

I'm fifty-six. The Obie-Wan Kenobi of our group. So the blonde hair is very much attributable to my hairdresser. I started graying in my forties and I don't even know how grey I am now. I am not about to let it grow out as I am sure that I would be completely depressed to see just how grey I am. This really falls under the heading of need to know. Not too bad in the wrinkle department, so far. I'm packing ten extra pounds, even with working out twice a week with a trainer who has sadist written all over his pretty little six-pack.

Lex is a widow. The other five are divorced. Some of us more than once. I tried twice. So I am two for two. Single looks very good to me now.

Our group has quite a bit in common. Maybe that is what brings us together. We are all instructors for Hudson River Community College. Four of us are in the English Department and two in the History Department. We are all single for six different reasons. And one of the best things about our little merry band of instructor BFFs is that we live within a short distance of teach other. Always a BFF ready to be there in the good times and especially in the difficult times.

I am the lucky owner of my house on the Hudson River because I bought it at the right time. The previous owners wanted to move to a condo and rid themselves of many issues that came with the house. Lots of issues.

I am sure that the only people who really find my house issues interesting are the "experts" at Home Depot. I think if I didn't show up at least twice on a weekend, they would send somebody to my house to check on me!

But it has been a safe haven and a blessing after my last divorce. Between school and the renovations on this house, there has been no time to feel sorry for myself.

I was just getting some potato skins ready to throw on my new little, handy, dandy George Forman Grill for after the troops arrived, when the first arrival rang the bell and charged in. It was Mora.

"Hey, what's up? You know, its probably a good thing we changed nights." Mora declared in her usual hard driving manner and her beautiful, Irish lilt. She didn't expect an answer. She handed me a bag from her favorite Irish pastry shop, I knew what would be in it. Gooey pastries and Irish rolls. Yum.

"I called everybody, they are on their way. Georgie is going to pick up Lex," she continued breathlessly, "So what's going on?" She grabbed two pillows off the couch and plopped her generous butt on the floor by the fireplace. She isn't fat. Just what the young guys call hot. We used to call it stacked.

Mora's fifty-one, looks ten years younger, acts younger than that. She's an exercise freak, goes to the gym everyday after her last class. Just thinking about it makes me tired.

Tiny frame with big boobs and the afore-mentioned great butt, she puts an hourglass to shame. Mora is a knockout. Flaming, thick, auburn hair that cascades in natural waves. She possesses the most perfect porcelain completion and her incredible emerald eyes flash with intelligence and passion. She is a woman who is comfortable with the world and her place in it.

She is one of the most sought after professors on our campus. She is popular with students not only because she is so knowledgeable but the is that she is able to get her students to want to learn and become involved. She has been the *State Small College Instructor Teacher of the Year* twice. Lex has had the same honor twice, as well. We have had several of our instructors from our campus earn that honor.

I'll never be *Teacher of the Year* or any other honor on campus. I am too abrasive and I piss of the administration quite regularly. The only reason that I do not get fired is that my classes fill up quite quickly and my students seem to like my style, what ever that is. I am not complaining.

Mora's not married but I don't know if she qualifies for single either. She has been in a long term relationship with her undertaker boyfriend for over twenty years.

We tease her about her inability to make up her mind but I think the reality is that both of them like the arrangement just fine the way it is. The rest of us seem to have on-again-off again relationships that suit us just fine too. I don't even know how many husbands and *friends* all of us have had because nobody really wants to count. For the most part we six, hot-flash BFFs, are at a very good place in our lives.

Just as I started to tell Mora about the reason for the change in nights, the doorbell chirped again and JJ and Regina burst in.

Neither JJ or Reg can just walk in calmly anywhere. They are BFFs and almost too much alike. They each have condos in the same building in Piermont. Both have Sealyham Terriers that are show dogs and much of their time outside of school is involved with AKC activities.   They are owner/handlers and are both close to achieving their championship points. Sometimes the two dogs even compete with each other but luckily, that has never been a problem.

The two dogs are really gorgeous and quite well behaved. And the rest of us support them by going to many of the local dog shows as we can. From little local dog shows to the big one. Every February we all troop into the City to go to the Westminster Dog Show. Just to watch. Their dogs have not gotten to that level and neither of them want to be that devoted or caught up in that fierce level of competition.

But the local dog shows are really a lot of fun for us. I can't count how many of the dogs shows and events that we go to. I am not really complaining. Somebody in the group calls and finds out who is available and off we go. It really is a fun, group hobby. The dogs love it too because it is an outing for them.

We are all dog people. Not a cat among us. Georgie has Herman, a beautiful little Westie. Mora has Rommel, the big guy in the group, a wonderful German Sheppard who was a shelter rescue. He was about a year old when she adopted him and that was about five years ago. Lex has two smooth-haired dachshunds, Beatrice and Benedict. Energetic, funny and great little lap dogs. She has shown both of them until they had their championship points. Now she breeds a littler every other year. Beatrice is only going to have one more litter and then she will just stud Benedict. This should make both dogs happy.

JJ was in the kitchen putting ice in glasses and yelling for Reg to come help her carry them into the living room when Georgie arrived with Lex.

Georgie took her seat primly in the high-back-chair. She is the lady in our group, quietly trying to point out good behavior to the rest of us. So far she is losing that battle. I think we all slip in little swear words just to see her pained expression.

Lex came out to the kitchen, gave me a quick hug and then helped carry bowls of chips I had been getting ready for our mass consumption.

One by one, each us grabbed an ice-filled glass and visited my well stocked bar to acquire a drink of choice.

I brought in an array of dips and settled into my usual place on my big comfy, chaise lounger, laughingly called the "grading station".

We are three sets of BFFs who have become a group of six friends. Good friends. We have been getting together for over twelve years. We have been through our good times and a whole lot of our bad times. Some really bad times. But we are all survivors. Thank goodness for a little help from our BFFs. Well, a lotta help!

We talk about everything and nothing, chatting easily with our usual genuine affection for each other. A big part of our survival is the laughter. Sometimes we become a veritable giggle fest. And we were doing it long before all the research came out about how laughing was therapeutically good for a person physically as well as mentally. I guess we are just cutting-edge-old-broads!

The door bell chimed and Mora squealed out, "FOOD!" as she jumped up to let Hai in. He lugged his bags into the dining room. He went to my highboy and took out plates, and other necessaries, set up the table for us, came back into the living room and said, "Ladies, dinner is ready". After getting his usual payment, he grinned at me, "See ya later, Professor Bell." gave his little happy-wave and scooted out the front door.

Hai is one of my best students. His family owns the Canton Wok and he has worked there since he was a kid. First one in the family to go to college. Great kid. Wish all my students had his work ethic. Too bad I can't find one just like he is to be my TA.

We all took our usual places around the table and began loading food onto our plates.

One of our great traditions, that we have developed over the years, is that we have sit-down dinners. We all have to go to too many activities that involve having to balance food on our knees and sit in awkward little groups and try to talk and keep from spilling everything on somebody's newly cleaned carpet. One of the real downsides of teaching is attending the rubber-chicken-circuit. Real table-talk works for us. I love our dinners. The only difference is that some do take-out like I do and the cooks in our group love to make lavish, and I admit, some scrumptious spreads.

Exactly one hour later, the door bell rang again; Hai came bouncing back in and while we returned to the living room, he cleared, cleaned, put away and then silently let himself out. Bless that boy! I pay him by the month for this, and many other food deliveries. I had also created a book fund for him with the book store. Someday, he will do great things with the education he is getting. Over the years, all six of us have done what we could to help deserving students. All six of us go to too many boring, civic events, far more than we would like, just to get the opportunity to talk to local businesses to get them to pony up money to help these kids. Our common passion is that education should not be for just the kids whose parents can open a wallet and an education flies out.

Once everyone had settled in their usual places and as we were concluding our unfinished dinner topics, I caught a lull and jumped in.

"O.K., Ladies, I have a plan." Five collective groans shot in my direction. "No, let me finish," I plunged on. "It's Friday, nobody has to get up early tomorrow, right? Usually we just segue from one topic to another. Tonight, let's have a little fun with the topics. Here are the rules."

Mora harrumphed, "Glory and her RULES!" JJ and Reg said, "Amen." at the same time. The other two just looked amused.

Not missing a beat I said, "One at a time, each of us will name a topic and then each of us will tell a story based on the topic. We are going to have a Canterbury Night. We are all teachers, right? Well, let's do what we tell the students to do. Present stories. We are going to present our own stories. Look at all of us. We are a collection of world literature, world history, and best of all, our own life experiences."

I rushed on, "We are all achievers, survivors, contributors, and we are the world's best sales people, at least in the classroom. One time, a fellow professor said to me that teachers were the ultimate sales people. Educators had to sell education to somebody who had no desire to acquire what you were selling. You had to make them want to buy your wares."

"So tonight, let's sell our wares!" Five sets of eyes looked at me with everything from amusement to downright horror.

Lex spoke first. "Well, it's my party and I'm game. Who else is in?"

Mora, warming to the topic, jumped up, clapped her hands as if she were starting class for an unruly bunch, looked at me, fire shooting out of her luminous green eyes, "Fine, if we are going to do this, then we will have to do it right. We all teach Chaucer both as literature and history so we all know the stories and the characters. We will use the same form. Chaucer never finished the return trip. So we will be the trip back with our stories. Everything has be told as a story, but a different style story. Beginning, middle, build-up, and ending. Characters, local color, the works!"

Georgie bubbled, "Yeah, this could be fun! My students tell stories every day, and I want to jump in and say, 'Excuse me, that's not how you tell a story.' I am so tired of certain words. We hear them every day, they write them in their papers. They decorate their note books with them! Doesn't anybody learn correct English anymore? What's worse is that they little turkeys get angry if you peg these words as being inappropriate or incorrectly used. I made a list one time and I had over one hundred of the most commonly written offensive and misued words. Spoken too. They give me a sharp pain right behind my eyes.

Georgie jumped up and began to gyrate as she spoke the works in a high teen-age-sing-song, *like,*

amazing,

the F word,

the B word,

the C word,

and I went,

so I says

pissed off,

Oh, good grief, there are just too many to list!"

Mora jumped back up and in her best teenage voice said, "I'se totally chillaxing with my Honeypot and OH EM GE, he goes 'let's just be friends with benefits', but he's trippin, WTF, Dude?" She bowed deeply to our appreciative laughter and applause.

Georgie added, "Any words used have to be part of the story and be specific. No generalities. No swear words unless they are part of the artistic integrity of the story." This brought on a good laugh from everybody.

Lex piped in, "So we can only use the F word if it furthers the story in a meaningful way." and winked at me.

Mora fluffed her top pillow and asked, "Who starts?"

Georgie looked at me and said, "Glory, this is your idea, you start. If I get the rules right, you set the first topic, tell the first story, we add to it by turns and then we go to the next topic. Correct?"

I shook my head yes.

Georgie continued, "Here's the line-up. Glory, Lex, Georgie, Mora, JJ, Reg. Everybody O.K with that?"

Lex looked at me. "Perfect. You're up, Sweet Cheeks! Name your topic and get us going."

The old adage flashed through my head: Be careful what you wish for, you might get it. Well, I just got it.

"Topic one. *The most influential person in your life.* Has to be human, can't be a pet, vegetable or mineral."

Mora, true to form, jumped up. "Let me start. I have been thinking about why I became a teacher. You all know my mother just died. I love you all for getting me through that. So let me start with her. I really think that it is all because of who and what she was."

Elizabeth Mary Bennett

She was the person who made all things possible in my family. My father, George Bennett was a Korean Vet. He was an Army Captain who came back in 1956 from Korea a very changed man. My mother said he was a bitter shell of the man whom she had married.

I was born in 1957 and he died in a car accident in 1958. I had two older brothers, born before my father went away to war.

Now she found herself with two boys, six and eight, and a one year old. The insurance was a joke and she had no alternative but to have to go out and make a living.

She started a daycare out of our house. My two brothers were even helpers with some of the little boys in her care. She would have anywhere between five and eight children to care for twelve hours a day, seven days a week. It was supposed to be six to six but often it was later because parents were always late picking up their kids.

I don't ever remember my mother complaining, ever being unhappy or in a bad mood. I am sure that she was but she sure did not ever let us see it. When I was eleven, she had saved enough money to buy the house next door and she turned that into a bigger care center.

She hired help and over time, she owned five centers in Nanuet, Nyack and New City. I think she could have been even bigger, owned more centers, but her focus was always on our family. She never forgot her own kids. We did things as a family as much as her crazy schedule would allow.

I know I just used to wonder what it would be like to have a father, but it wasn't something that I obsessed over. My life was always good.

My brothers turned out well, Mickey is a social worker, I guess because he was around kids so much. Conn took over the centers when Mother retired.

Here is the sad part. Until about ten years ago, I just took all that she did as my entitlement. I never appreciated a damn thing she did for me. And yes, the "damn" is part of my story development.

Mom was a warm, good-looking woman. I sure that there were opportunities for her to have met somebody and had a life after my father's death but I just took for granted that she didn't want anything else. She took care of us and worked. That was it. What a selfish little beast I was. Damn, yeah, said it again. Society really does a job on women doesn't it?

We have to make all the choices that men don't. I'll bet if it had been the other way around, my father would have remarried, and we would have become extras in his life.

Mom made every sacrifice to raise us. Why does it take so long for us to see what they really do?

One time a friend of mine told me that she never got what her mother had given up and sacrificed for her until her own two kids dumped all over her.

Her husband left her for a man. He burst out of the closet. Her two boys asked her what she had done to make him that way. And her ex-hubby reinforced that idea with a made-up story about her having an affair and it turned him against women.   Wonder how long it will take these two little toads to get the real picture? I know, I know, I'm man bashing.

Yes, I get that there are many good men out there. I just happen to be one of those people that has not encountered that many.   But, I digress.

Remember, last year when I went to New Jersey? I went to see my dad's brother. I wanted to know more about my father. Uncle Jack is eighty-one. He was my dad's older brother. Anyway, he told me some family history that I never knew.

I guess Dad was a charmer.   Too charming. When he had the accident there had been a woman in the car with him. I rattled the family tree and guess what fell out?

I became a teacher because I saw how Mother affected so many lives. She did not just warehouse kids. She taught them. She cherished them. I think I adopted my kids because of her influence. I know that has to do with her too. I also think of my students as my legacy and by extension, her legacy.

I know I don't get to *fix* that many of of my students. But there are those that where we do get to make a difference and that just reinforces why I am a teacher. I know it is corny, but we all know that we could double, even triple our salaries if we used our education in another

career. But how do you put a price on being that
one person that a kid needs to change his or her
world. We all have those stories. Kind of a notch
on our student success belt.

My influence is still my mother. I can feel
her channeling through me and smiling every time
I do have a success with one of the students."

Oh, good grief, I didn't mean to get so
serious about this. I promise, my next story will
be funny. Well, I hope it will be funny.

Georgie patted Mora's hand as she plopped back down
on her pillows. Then she handed her a tissue and the rest of us
sat in a comfortable silence all of us lost in thoughts of "the
might-have-beens".

Finally I broke the silence and said, "Well, if we are
going to keep the order, that would make it JJ's turn."

JJ shook her head as if she was clearing out what she
was thinking. "Wow, to me huh? All right, Here is my story.
It's a grim fairytale."

The Orphans

Once upon a time there was a mother, a
father and four little offspring all running amuck.

The mother and father had a taste for the fermented grape and most of the time, they forgot that they had made four little ones who needed feeding and nurturing in order to grow big and strong.

Tim, the oldest, left home at thirteen and no one seemed to care or want to look to see where he had gone. And over time everybody forgot that there had been a Tim.

June, the next oldest, tried her very best to take care of the family. The mother and father would put the remaining three children in the back of the old Plymouth, and drive to the local roadhouse. The children would sit in the back of the car for hours. June would use old towels for diapers to try to keep baby Ollie dry and clean.

Sometimes kind bar patrons would feel sorry for this sad little collection of lost children and they would take them a sandwich or sodas and sometimes even a milkshake that the children would gratefully share.

Other times the children were left at home for days with no food, horrific housing conditions and only each other for comfort.

One day when the children were home alone, a shinny black car drove up to the ramshackle dwelling they called a home.

Two men in dark blue suits and a grey suited lady came up on the porch and asked where the parents were. June was trying to push Jane and Ollie behind her, and she told the woman that her parents had gone to town but would be coming back in a little while.

The woman said her name was Mrs. James and she was from an agency in town. The children did not know what an agency was. She opened the torn and tattered screen door, reached past June, pulled Ollie from behind June and handed him to one of the men who took him to the shinny car, then she pulled Jane away and handed her to the other man and Jane was put into the car next to Ollie. Then Mrs. James took June by her hand and added her into the car as well. Mrs. James sat in the back with the shaking, huddled children.

They went back toward the town but did not stop there. They traveled much further, and each child was taken to a different place. June went to a big, grey building, Ollie went to big, brick building, and Jane was taken to a children's hospital. None of the children had uttered a sound in the car or when the were pulled from the only life they had known and thrust into a future without their only comfort of each other.

The children were now separated from one another permanently and each did not know where the other siblings were or why their parents did not come get them.

Jane was at the hospital for a very long time. One day she asked a nurse what was wrong with her and the nurse said kindly, that her lungs did not work as well as they should. But that she was getting better and stronger every day. Finally one day they told her she was going to leave the hospital and go to another place to live.

Jane was taken to an orphanage where many people came to take children and adopt them. But Jane was never picked until one day when Jane was fourteen, an older couple came and sat and talked with Jane. They asked her if she wanted to go live with them. Jane did not even know what to answer. She did not know if it would be better or worse than what she had.

The couple suggested that she try it for a few weeks and if Jane would want to stay with them she could. So that is what happened. It took Jane a long time to realize that she had a family who loved her and even longer to trust herself to have feelings. But eventually she did.

Jane discovered that she loved to read, to write and that she loved to read to others and talk about what she had learned. She wanted to share all the exciting things that she had discovered.

Jane's new, wonderful mother asked her one day if she wanted to go to college. Jane had to think about it. College had never seemed like a possibility to her. Then she said, 'Yes, I could try it.' At the college, a wonderful professor gave her the opportunity to learn about all of the great literature of the world and one day, that professor said, 'Jane, do you know that you could be a professor too? And you could continue to create possibilities for others to learn about all of the great literature of the world.'

Jane was thrilled. And that is exactly what she did. But the story has another happy ending. She worked with a magical company that knew how to find lost people.

One day, she had a phone call and it was from her sister, June. June, and Jane got together and had a very happy reunion. And together they looked and looked and found out that Ollie lived in the far away state of Pennsylvania and he traveled for a very long way and they all got together and were all very happy. They promised each other that they would never be lost from each other ever again.

So, Jane cannot just pick one person. It would have to be her new mother and father who came to save her from the horrible school, and the professor who taught her what she could be.

Jane has lived reasonably happy life to this day.

There was not a dry eye in our group. We had known that Jane was adopted but most of us had not known the story behind the adoption.

Reg said, "JJ told me some of this but it was her past so it was hers to tell. I guess this was the right time."

JJ said, "Well, I need a refresher". And she went to the bar and refilled her glass.

Reg asked the group, "Well, how is the world do I top that? Well, I do have one. This is a teeny-tiny little taste a book I am working on. I am trying to write the biography of this incredible woman and influence on my life. The hard part is that all of my memories of her are from my childhood. But here goes."

Johanna May Beliks

Meeting Johanna was a happy accident. I was on my way home from school one wonderful, sparkly, May day. I was having happy thoughts about the last day of school which was just around the corner.

I had seen and spoken to her on several occasions. She was always cheerful and would make a comment about the weather or some comment about my pretty braids or what I was wearing.

This particular day she asked me if I could do a chore for her. I said, "Of course,' and climbed the stairs to her porch. I entered a greenery shrouded, lusciously cool, fragrant little oasis with honeysuckle and climbing-rose-covered lattices. I felt as if I had stepped into a different world. And I had.

I said, "How are you doing, Mrs. Belkis?" And she said, "Oh, Regina, you can call me

Johanna." I was surprised that she knew my name. But then it was a small town and everybody knew everybody.

She asked me if I wanted to earn a quarter a week. I told her I would be happy to do whatever she needed. She said that she had a girl who did housework for her but she would not clean the cat box. It was getting difficult for her to do it herself. I told her that was easy and I would do it when ever she needed it. She said that twice a week would be better because it 'could get pretty stinky.' Just then a giant, orange, tabby cat slowly climbed onto the porch, made a great leap and landed in Johanna's lap where he stayed. Johanna said his name was Major.

Johanna, herself, was shabby and elegant at the same time. She was layered like an old artichoke. What I could not see I could imagine. She wore old, thick stockings with seams that pointed every direction except up and down. On top of the stockings, she wore droopy ankle socks that were shapeless from many washings.

She sported serviceable, old, clunky, brown shoes that laced up the front. A white slip peeped out from under a dark, crepe dress. She was never without a wool sweater about her frail shoulders. And she buttoned this sweater with one button right in the middle even on the hottest of days. All together she looked like a once elegant old mansion, which had been lived in, cherished, and still was much loved.

Her face was a treasure of angles and lines. I was always fascinated by her eyes. I knew that she had seen a world that I was only beginning to imagine.

What started out to be a twice weekly thing, quickly became an every day visit. She used to watch for me from the massive old rocker that her father had brought from Poland somewhere around 1800.

It turned out that Major's cat box was just a cardboard box filled with dirt from her back yard. I got my dad to get several bags of sand from the lumber yard and put them under the back porch. He got a short, galvanized tub that became major's new cat box. Dad also got me a little garden rake to scrape the icky from the sand. I learned how to do a cat box cleaning.

Her house was always cool and dark. It was dingy with age and neglect, but it was a happy place. I loved being with this incredible person who so clearly loved me and loved being with me.

Johanna had been a nurse in World War I. Her exciting stories took me to the front lines and to the people of Italy and France.

After the war she had become a teacher. She said that she had had enough of death and dying and she wanted to work with young people who were the future of the world and because she wanted to be around youth and energy.

She and I would read from her books. We would read Twain, Dickens and especially from so many of the women authors, Mary Shelly's, *Frankenstein*, Eliot's, *Silas Marner* and all of the Bronte books. Because of her, I was reading the classics when my school mates were discovering Nancy Drew.

She introduced me to real tragedy. Her husband had been a mining engineer who had lost his life in a mining accident and her only child, a boy, had died from diphtheria.

Johanna has given me the gift of pride. She had a fierce, abiding confidence in herself, women in general and me in particular.

I know that because of Johanna I am better able to deal with my problems. She has helped me to understand that it was more about the problems that my mother had and her drinking was really not about me. She told me that my mother had inner demons that were as much a problem for her as they were for me, maybe more.

She used to say I would understand a lot more when I was older. One of her favorite sayings was, 'Every time you learn something from a problem, the next one is easier.' Another was, Forgiving someone does wonders for the forgiver. Well, it does. I have learned to understand my mother and forgive her.

She used to tell me I could do anything, be anything, I just needed to prepare myself with the fundamentals of education and determination.

And best of all she connected me to a world that had passed on by.

I had just begun a romance with the Civil War novels. Johanna told be that she had been born a few years before the surrender of Lee to Grant and I was enthralled.

Her stories were my first person guide and magic carpet to an era that I could only visit through her stories. She had been there, she had lived in this exciting time gone by.

She told me stories about Prohibition, flappers, presidents from Cleveland to Truman and stories of both World Wars.

She died at ninety-six. Major had died the year before.

When days are tough for me, I think of Johanna. She was a gentle, prideful, beautiful woman who has become an angel who sits on my shoulder. She will always be there.

She is for all time, my Johanna May Belkis. She was my role model for becoming a teacher.

And that, my dear ladies of higher learning, is my most influential person. So I hope you can see why I am trying to turn this lovely memory into a book. I want the world to know this woman as I did. Now I yield the floor. Over to you Lex."

Lex said, "I have an influential one too. It's a teacher story. Some of you know my back story. I had a troubled childhood and spent my early years in school acting out. This was my turn-around experience.

My epiphany

The source of my epiphany was my eighth-grade English teacher. I was having a tough time at home. I am not going to rehash that, at least not right now, I am just presenting about an influential, life changing incident. It still amazes me that something that short in duration could have such long term ramifications on my life.

I had been acting out in class. The usual. One day I must have really gotten going. I know that Mrs. Clark had tried to deal with me. It was my second year with her. When she moved from teaching seventh to eighth English, she had asked to have me in her class again.   Normally I was not that much of a problem in her class. Fortunately for this problem kid, Yours Truly, she was the one teacher I connected with and I loved her classroom for so many reasons.

She was well aware that I did not want to go home before my father got home, so I would stay after school to help her clean the chalk boards, grade papers, and help tidy the classroom. It was years later when I realized that she put in those extra hours to protect me from the horror that I was enduring at home. Which is its own story for a later time.

I was a regular in the principal's office from other classes, but Mrs. Clark was a true teacher as well as a master of knowing what a student needed. She used to try to distract me, and if all else failed she would tell me to take a book and go read outside. I truly loved this woman and I did not understand why I would act out in her class.

I know, imagine sending a student outside to read and get under control today? Anyway, this day, I must have pushed all of her buttons.

She walked over to my desk, and said in a very quiet, firm voice, but one that left no doubt about its intent. 'Alexandria, go wait out by the lockers, I will be there in a minute.'

I went out, and stood there wondering if she was going to send me to the principal or worse. I wasn't sure what worse was. She rarely used my full name. So this gave me a clue I had pushed too far.

After what seemed like a long time, she came out and stood in front of me. I was taller as she was a tiny woman, but for the first time, she actually scared me.

'I have had all of your nonsense!' she began. She was not yelling, it was worse than yelling. She was looking at me with the same eyes and speaking in the same voice that I know all of us have used, when we are frustrated and trying to make a kid understand something that is far more important than the content we are teaching.

'You are not learning. Not a thing! You are so busy being angry and distracting me and everybody in the classroom, that I can't teach, you can't learn and nobody else can either.'

'So, your mother is winning. If that is what you want, just keep acting this way. If not, get yourself, your emotions and your brain under control. You can't fix anybody but yourself. You have one of the best brains to come through my classes in years. And you are throwing it away. I understand why, I really do, but that does not change what you need to do to help yourself.

Now stay out here and think about it. When you are ready to be a student come back in.

If not, go to the office for the rest of the period, because I don't want to deal with your crap anymore.

She got quiet and looked at me for a few minutes, then turned on her heel and walked back into the classroom.

I walked to the edge of the little center park and sat under a tree. I was having a major epiphany. Big time.

My mother was winning? Well that really was crap. I was not going to let that happen. And I was not learning? I wasn't going to let that happen either. Understanding just kept coming. I knew that Mrs. Clark really cared. So why was I fighting her or ruining her classroom?

Just as I started back into the classroom, the bell rang. I let everybody leave the room and walked up to her desk.

Neither of us said a word. I just looked at her, she stood up, gave me a quick hug and gently turned me toward the door.

That was the day I became a real learner. And I know that Mrs. Clark is why I became a teacher. I wanted to be that person who made somebody have that flash of awareness. Someone who had the possibility of changing the trajectory of a life for the better.

But hey, can anybody change the topic? I want to hear something funny!

Reg jumped up, "Hey, I know it is not my turn but I have a goofy one and it's quick. Believe me it has nothing to do with an influential person. Trust me, I got some funny! Just to change the pace. I know, off topic just like our students."

Preggers Faux Pas

I was pregnant with kid number two, Aubrey. About eight months. I had to go in for those horrible weekly check ups because of some minor problems.

So I am up in the torture chamber, feet stuck in the steel traps and spread-eagled. The doctor is in position and he asks me a question, just as I get ready to answer, I have to sneeze. But that is not all I do. I let out the longest and loudest fart of my life. It is majorly epic. I outdid myself. And I am sad to admit, this one smelled worst than the New Jersey Landfill. I have no idea why. My eyes water just remembering it.

The doctor raises up to where I can just see his dazed look, so I know that I have done something so spectacular that it has even surpassed his usual clientele. Remember, the offending part of my anatomy is inches from his nose.

The poor doctor finished up what he had to do, stood up, still looking dazed, patted me on the arm, and without a word, scooted out the door.

Hoping I could escape without seeing anyone, I dressed as quickly as I could and I scuttled out the room, just as the nurse was coming in with a can of Glade. I wondered if there was a special fragrance for my transgression.

All I could think about for the rest of that pregnancy was that I had to do at least three more, awkward, appointments. I don't know how I did it, but I did get through them even though I was so panicked each time that I would have to sneeze or cough and it would be smellville all over again. I wondered if the doc were bracing himself for another possible meltdown.

The doctor never mentioned my faux pas, and of course, I never said anything either. Fortunately, after Aubrey was born, I never had to see that doctor again.

Regie finished to a great round of applause from all of us.

JJ said, "I hear fart stories every day. Some of my students even think that it makes a good paper topic, but that is one of the best fart stories I have ever heard! But trust me if you ever run into him he will never know who you are. One time I was having lunch with a friend, and I saw my OBGYN sitting at the next table. I gave a little wave and he looked at me as if I just got off a space ship. My friend said, 'He didn't recognize you with your clothes on!'"

JJ made a horn of her hands and did the Ta Da! thing, "You do realize that we are not staying on topic. Who cares? If something reminds us of a story let's just go for it."

With some very pointed looks at me and everybody shaking their well coifed heads affirmatively, I agreed. It was going to be our usual crap shoot of topics. Oh, well.

"Glory Girl, you are it."

I stood up and faced my judges.

"Mine goes back to when the twins were pre-teen. They had just turned twelve. Truman had not done his little

Houdini thing yet. He had just made partner at the firm and we were having our first home entertaining, a dinner for one of the other partners. I was very nervous about planning a formal evening for a senior partner who had married a much younger trophy wife and their child, Benny who was ten. I asked my older kids to be there too to show what a solid, normal family we were. Yeah, I know, I didn't think that one through! "

Mama's Boy

The twins had tried unsuccessfully to engage this kid in some rambunctious boy activities before dinner but the he had stayed glued to his mother all the while we were having pre-dinner drinks. They tried enticing him with computer games that they didn't even let anybody else play but them. No go.

This dinner was such a big deal, that Truman had suggested that I hire both a cook and a maid to serve. With my lack of cooking skills it seemed like a good idea. So the maid came to the living room door and announced dinner.

We all trooped into the dinning room, everybody took their seats. Benny was in between his mom and dad.

Somehow the discussion involved the mother's devotion to this strange child. The dad mentioned that Mom gave Benny his nightly bath. The works.

Casey and Connor sat with their mouths hanging open at the idea of a mother bathing somebody their age.

As the meal progressed, Benny's mother cut up his food and then began to supply a forkfull at a time to his little birdie-beak of a mouth.

Then Casey and Connor began to feed each other. That was not enough for them. They began a dialog, *'Oh, Casey, let me give you some of this wonderful salad.'* *'Oh, Connor, look at this tasty roast beef.'* *'Have a little bite for me.'* *'Oh, what a good boy.'*

The father caught on very quickly and even had the good grace to get that it was funny.

He probably was not any more comfortable with the way the mom babied the kid than we were watching it.

Truman was horrified and told the boys to stop. They didn't.

Finally the mother came out of her fog, became aware of the mockery and said to my two miscreants, 'Boys, that is not very nice. Bennie is a different kind of boy.'

Well, my kids got the *different* part. Bennie's dad got that. I got that. The only one who didn't was poor, deluded mom.

Needless to say, that was the only formal dinner at our house.

Truman left shortly after that for his own trophy wife.

Life goes on. But from then on, at every Sunday dinner and now when both twins wind up at the house at the same time, one of the little tunas feeds the other one and we all fall on the floor laughing. For some damn reason, it never stops being funny. Embarrassing at the time, but always funny.

What has always made it even funnier for me was that Truman never got why it was funny.

JJ was smothering a giggling fit as she said, "Oh, Glory, that is one dinner I would have paid to see. I have met Mr. Tight-Ass Truman, and I can just see him all puffed up and embarrassed. You dodged a bullet when you got rid of that prig. Sorry Gorgie, But I calls 'em as I sees 'em. And I even cleaned up the last part."   And even Gorgie smiled benevolently at all of us, forgiving our language transgressions.

I looked over at Lex. "Lex, you're batting cleanup." Lex looked thoughtful. "Well, mine is definitely embarrassing, but it's not funny."

A Gift of Compassion

I was twelve.   My cousin Shelia was visiting and Dad had taken us to the Nanuet Mall. We were in Macy's and running around chasing each other. Shelia had ducked behind a clothing rack and I yelled at her. 'Come out, you retard!' Just then a woman pushing a large baby stroller with a child who looked four or five, with very obvious Downs Syndrome, came around the rack toward me.

She looked totally stricken and I was mortified. I burst into tears, and she reached over to comfort me which just made me cry harder. My dad arrived to pick us up just then, and as he walked up and he assumed that something had happened to me. He asked me if I were hurt.

I couldn't answer because I was crying so hard.   The woman said, 'She will tell you what happened later. But tell her that I understand, and this will be a lesson for her.' Of course my father was totally puzzled. It was after we were almost home before I could tell him what happened.

Dad said the same thing the woman had. 'Lexie, you just learned a very important lesson. Words can hurt people. Labels hurt people. The woman showed you what true compassion is. Now, use what you learned and don't beat yourself up about it.'

Look, that was almost forty years ago, and I am still ashamed. But it taught me what true compassion is. She was a very gracious lady. I wish I had known her name. I would like to have spoken to her and thanked her for that lesson.

We were all very quiet. Each of us was thinking about our own times of saying the wrong thing at the wrong time.

Mora finally spoke. "You know, I think about that all the time. I know I tend to be somewhat sarcastic and I say things and then I wonder if I have offended a student. I don't mean anything, but you know, they sometimes hear something different from what we say."

JJ said, "Hear, Hear! I think about that too. Just last week a girl wrote me a note and asked me what I meant about something. I didn't even remember what I had said, and I had to call in her for a conference to clear it up. She repeated my statement. I had been talking about women having choices. She heard something so different from what I meant. Somehow her perception was that I was devaluing women if they chose to be a stay-at-home mother. Of course she had a stay-at-home mother, and she thought I was being negative about that choice."

"We are English teachers, well except for Georgia and Mora, you two, poor, history teachers. We all know how communication screws everybody up. Just like the old song, Masquerade. Sums up all major lit themes. You all know the line: *We tried to talk it over but words got in the way.*"

We were all nodding. Regina added, "Yeah, been there, done that. I just finished a book that talked about the idea that communication was the beginning of mankind's inability to bond. Strange idea but I still get the premise."

We all sat quietly, reflecting on private thoughts.

Mora broke the silence. "How about a round of *How I Met a Significant Other*. I got a couple of good ones! HA! But first, is anybody hungry? I will spring for a couple of pies if anybody else is looking for a midnight repast. Dartella's makes a mean pie. I'm thinking three pies, the works." A few nods from the group and she made a mad dash for the phone.

I said, "Okey Dokey, let's chill until after we eat. Lex, come help me set up the table."

11:46 PM

"Hey," I told her as we walked to the kitchen, "I just got some designer paper-plates and silver plastic-ware. Is that a contradiction in terms or what? Designer plastic.   I swear, it is silver colored. Hilarious. As if somebody could mistake them for real silverware!"

Thirty minutes later, our next dinner bell rang. Lex opened the door, snatched the boxes from the poor, startled delivery guy, gave the him his money with a generous tip, then she almost shoved the poor kid out the door. I gave her a quizzical look because she is usually so mild mannered. Lex shrugged and said, "I'm tired, I'm hungry, so sue me!"

JJ laughed, and said, "Maybe just a little PMS? Fortunately Lex thought her remark was funny. Could have gone either way.   I was beginning to understand the reason for Lex's mood swings and anxiety. But I sure as Hell wasn't going to point it out. Even as BFFs, that did not fall in my job description. I would encourage a trip to the gyno but that was it. No way was I going to point out her new mood shifts or what I thought. I wondered if she had had her first hot flash yet.

Sometimes I really wonder about old mother nature. We have the joy of having the miracle of bringing the new generation into the world but we pay for it with the monthlies and all that goes with them and then we go through the drenched sheets, the unexpected heat rush at the most inopportune times and all that goes with that whole process that announces to us that we are entering an entirely surprising, new phase of the life cycle. Lex has been the last of our group to enter this unwanted club.

The smell of the aromatic pizza chased the thoughts from my mind as it beckoned us to the dining room. Frankly it did not take much encouragement. Mice in a maze with a promise of a wad of cheese had nothing on us.

We all took our places around the table and fell in to eating like a pack of ravenous wolves. Nobody makes a better pizza.

For a few, very comfortable minutes, nobody spoke, just a lot of chewing and sighing. Finally Lex said, "Well, there's three, dead soldiers, let's bury the boxes and clear the table. Oh, how I love a meal where the only cleanup needed is a trash can!"

We all made side trips to the bathroom then trooped back into the living room and JJ was talking about a new training program that the college was imposing on all of the faculty. We kicked around the merits and the drawbacks and determined that it was another "feel good program" that would just be one more time-waster and another certificate in our files.

"Come on my Fellow Imparters of Great Knowledge," Lex teased, "Let's get this party back on track. I like this topic. I have a doozy. World class! Olympic winner! Want me to go first or do we start with *Glory's list* again?"

Georgie pointed at Lex, "Hell yes, you start. Sounds intriguing. I sit here ready to be entertained and enlightened." All eyes looked at Lex and she began.

"All of you know about my cop." This brought on a chorus of groans from the group. "No", she protested. "You guys always judge him. Remember that's my job," she chided the group gently.

Georgie scooted around on her knees, grabbed Lex around the waist and said, "Sorry, you know I love you so much I just want to wrap you up and screen all your relationships. We all do. That's our job." Lex patted Gorgie's head and said, "OK, scooch back and give me room. This is a big story!"

Georgie rolled her eyes. I glared.   Lex pretended not to notice.

"Janine was in her first year at Dominican. So that would make it November of 2003. Remember, she did not want to go where I was teaching. Already she was showing her independence."

"Damn, I didn't know you had been seeing Hunter that long!" JJ burst out. "Oh, sorry, I'll be quiet." and she zipped her lips and threw the *key* at Mora who caught the *air key*.

The Flat Tire

Janine had only been at school a couple of months and she was working at a Quick Pick. She got off at 2 A.M when it closed.

I had tried to talk her out of working there because it scared me silly. I used to go wait in the parking lot for her and follow her home. Well, that only lasted for a while and then she put on her big-girl pants and told Mom to let her be a grown up.

This brought a combination of groans and sighs from the group.   Lex shushed everybody and continued,

Harvey had died only two years before, and I knew I was smothering both Janine and

Austin. But I knew that this job had a crapload of built-in dangers.

There had been instances of workers being robbed, followed, and worse for years and it wasn't getting better.   But we all know eighteen-year-olds. It can't happen to them; they know everything. I tried being discreet and following her for several nights, but she figured it out.

So I had to put on *my big-girl pants* and let her do her thing. Austin had just gotten his license and he tried to bargain with her but she rejected that too. The only good part was that there were two girls on that late shift.

I could never sleep until she got home. One Friday night, the phone rang at 2:36. She should have already been home and I was getting Antsy. I picked up the phone, read the readout and it was not her cell, but was a number I didn't know. So I was very surprised when I heard her voice.

'Mom, can you come get me?'

'Why?' I asked, 'Where are you?'

'I am at the Stony Point Roadhouse.'

'You are where?' I shrieked. 'WHY?'

'Because I had a flat tire.'

'Wait, number one, why would you be in Stony Point at the Roadhouse, that's six miles from here? Two, if you had a flat why are you calling from the Roadhouse? Three, where is your cell?'

'Well, first, my cell is not charged, I forgot to bring my charger with me. Second, I had to give Beverly a ride home and I got a flat, third, I stopped at the station next to the Roadhouse and the guy wouldn't fix my flat because he was closing up. So I had to come over here to use the phone. I was hoping that I would see somebody from school and they could give me a ride.'

'Mom, stop asking questions and just come get me. I'll be out front.' And she hung up before I could tell her to stay inside.

I scrambled out of bed, put on sweats, grabbed a jacket out of the hall closet, rammed my car out of the garage and went roaring out of the neighborhood.

I broke the speed limit just hoping a cop would follow me or stop me because I wanted documentation about the jerk who would not change her tire. I vaguely knew there was some kind of city ordinance about having to give service in emergency situations.

By now it was after 3 A.M. when I went screeching into the jammed parking lot, spewing gravel and pulled up in front. There she was, standing by the bar sign all by herself. A shock of fear shot through me.

She was so vulnerable and I realized just how helpless we become to protect them when they make these unthinking decisions. I am sure the thoughts running through my head were not quite that lucid. But that's the gist of it.

She tumbled into the car, and it was all I could do not to grab her, hug her first and then shake the daylights out of her.

She pointed to the gas station next to the roadhouse. 'That's the jerk who would not change my tire.'

I could see a light on inside. I pulled the car in front and jumped out. I started banging on the door. A young guy, twentyish, came toward the door, making closed gestures and pointing to the sign to confirm it.

By now I am screaming like a mad woman. 'Open the damn door!'

He yells out, 'Go away or I'm callin' a cop!'

'Do it! You little turd,' I yell.

Now Jeanine is out of the car trying to pull me away. 'Mom, let's just go home.'

So the aforementioned little turd calls 911! I see him dial it. OK, then. Bring it on!

So I push Jeanine back into the car and we sit and wait. A Black and White from Stony Point's Finest pulls up. Two Uniforms get out. The older one comes over to the car, to my open window. 'Well, Ladies, what's up?'

Now here comes the part where I don't want any of you making rude noises or comments.

I could feel the electricity in the air and I just kept looking at this great looking cop. He was obviously looking back. Turns out, as you know, he was a detective who also did rookie training and he was working with a newbie.

End of the "tire" story, the owner of the station was fined because the kid had refused to change her tire and Janine had pulled into the gas station at least fifteen minutes before they actually closed.

Hunter called me the next day. Asked me if we were both OK after our *ordeal*. We went out for coffee and now we had been hit-and-miss after all these years.   It been an odd connection. Certainly physical. But we were also connect by the fact that we had childhood demons and quirky personalities.   For the most part we got each other. And I can never fault him about how he treated the kids. It was a good connection there too. They still like and respect him. And he has been there for them with out the smothering.

JJ let out another exasperated sigh, Lex turned to her,

JJ, don't get your panties in a wad. He told me the very first time we went for coffee that he was married but separated. They still are separated. I doubt if that will ever change. She is Catholic and she likes her life just the way it is.

A couple of years ago he asked me if I wanted to get married. He was willing to get a divorce. I did a bucket-load of soul searching and thinking about what I wanted.

I realized that I don't have any desire to get married and be a fulltime wife. I like knowing that if I get a bellyful, I can just say 'I've had it, go away'. I wonder how many women, maybe men too, get married just to prove something. Sometimes it is just an ego thing.

I had the good solid man with Harvey. We had almost twenty-one years. Mushy, hokey, whatever you want to call it, we had as close to perfect a relationship as it gets. I don't think that kind of lightning strikes twice.

So now what I had with Hunter had worked for me. And it worked for quite a while. You all see Hunter as the bad guy. He is and he isn't. I, know, great ambiguity for a teacher.

So, I guess I might as well tell you now, that I am ending it. It is just one of those things that has run its course. We have both figured out that what was good and what was working is not working anymore. But it is one of those things that I had to figure out for myself.

I wish that life were so simple that somebody could say, 'Oh, that situation is not good for you.' And we could agree and move on. Life is not like that. Look how many times we have thought somebody had a great marriage and then a short time later they are split. Too many factors come into play.

I'm sure we are doing a round of *Crappy Things My Man Has Done.* Hunter has finally made me see that it is a no-win for either of us. We have had seven years. But now the bad is outweighing the good. But I had to see it. Funny, we complain that the kids make stupid, uniformed decisions. Well, we adults do too. But I am working on getting informed! And I am trying to make better decisions.

Now, don't give me any sympathy and let's get on with the next story. But, before we do that, Glory, where's the cotton-pickin' chocolate? I know you have a stash around here somewhere.

2:37 AM

Five pairs of eyes were looking at me with unbridled greed. I walked over to the highboy and pulled out a two-pound box of Godiva Chocolates and the group fell upon it; in minutes, there were scattered, empty, reminders of the endorphin inducing little, brown spheres of mindless goodness. A few more minutes and the box was a sad, empty hull.

Mora sighed, "You know, I really must be getting old because I think I would rather have chocolate than almost any other experience. Hell, for me it is an experience!"

This elicited a round of nodding and everything from a giggle to Mora's lovely, throaty, laugh. How she could make the sounds she did and spill out music was magical. She did nothing half way.

Six women, two pounds of little pleasure inducing spheres. You do the math!

Two pounds of Godiva Chocolates vanished into that world where all good chocolates go. Sometimes I am amazed that we all eat the way we do and yet none of us are really that heavy. We are not lightweights, but for our ages, we are reasonably fit. But then we do work at it in our own fashion.

We all knew we would pay for our night of eating debauchery but it was not something we did all the time. Birthdays, and some holidays were always our excuse to indulge.

Five pairs of eyes turned to me again. Easy to read; asking what else I had. Well, there was a goody.

"Mora, come help me." I went to the second fridge in my pantry, and voila! I pulled out the incredible, edible birthday cake that I had ordered and stashed.

I had ordered it a week ago. And the bakery in Nyack had done an fantastic job. It had cost a fortune but this masterpiece was worth it. Sometimes I need to be reminded that art comes in so many forms from so many imaginations.

The cake was the shape of an open book, and they had made figures that looked as if they were escaping from the open pages of this book. Shakespeare, one of the Brontes, Hawthorne, Hemingway, and several others. Other figures were all around the sides. I had taken pictures of it for the book that I was going to make for Lex.

Inside, it was luscious, gooey, chocolate amaretto, and the three layers had two fillings. One strawberry-almond-amaretto, the other was truffle and raspberry jam supreme.

I had decided not to put any candles on the cake itself. It is such a work of art that candles should not detract from these beautifully done, imaginative pieces. Literature as edible art. Mara and I went into the dining room and put several of my crystal candle holders on either side of the cake. Lex really did not need a reminder of the number of years she has racked up. In reality, there are not that many but this just happens to be the year that she has had that T.S. Eliot feeling of life passing by. I know that she will get over it. Most of us do.

Suddenly, I was thinking about my panic year. I had been much younger. Still married to hubby number one, Col. I was in my *Miss Suzie Homemaker* phase. Of course, that phase had been going on for all of my marriage. I was still in that mindset that if I cooked fabulous meals, sewed all our clothes, baked bread and pastries, and did everything I was told, one day Col would turn into the prince that I thought I had married. So far that hadn't happened.

It was my 29th birthday. I had a tough day at school. Oh, there were the usual little gifts from the students. And I did value that.   The usual lunch in the faculty lounge, cake and all. But I had to council with a student that I really had been working with who was on the drop-out track and she told me that day that it would be her last day at the college. I tried to reason with her. I used all the arguments that I could muster, and finally she broke down, and through gales of tears, she hiccupped out that she was pregnant, And it got worse. The father of her baby was married and told her to get lost. Her own parents had told her to leave their home, that they were ashamed and would no longer support her. I never cease to be amazed at how humans can hurt those they profess to love when love is needed the most.

Of course that evening I just knew that I needed to try to do something to get her counseling, to help her find a place to live, to get her back in school.

I wish that it had a happy ending but it didn't. She committed suicide just a few months later. I carried the guilt that I could have done something, said something, used the right words. I had tried to find her. She just dropped out of sight. I still carry the feeling that I should have done something.

But the day of my birthday was tough, trying to sort through how I could help this lost child. It was the first time I become entwined in a students problems that were beyond academic. I spent several hours running around campus trying to find out which avenue would be the best to try to help her. There were resources and I was making lists of who and how to help her. My emotions were on a rollercoaster or hope and despair. Worse yet, I was feeling so inadequate. Reality had snuck up and smacked me right across the chops. School was the one place where I always felt very confident. I didn't that day.

That evening I needed Col. Not a present, not a cake or a party. That certainly wasn't Col's style. I needed somebody that cared about me enough to let me talk about my frustrations and sadness over this situation. I needed to know that I mattered.

Col did not come in until almost nine. Of course the kids were in bed. But I had made a nice dinner and held it warm. I wanted some acknowledgement that I mattered to him. Not a word about my birthday, not a 'How was your day? Nada!

I said, with what I hoped was a bright, cherry tone. 'Sit down, I'll get our dinner. I made something special.' He barely glanced at me and spit out, 'Never mind, I already grabbed a hamburger. Listen, I'm beat. I'm crashing.' He turned on his heel and walked out of the room.

I crashed too. All the way. I was so upset that I needed to clean. After a couple of hours of cleaning, I was up on a kitchen ladder with my head stuck in a cabinet, cleaning something that was not really dirty to begin with and suddenly I had my epiphany. In ten years, who would care about the cleaning, the laundry, the baking, the shinny floors? And most of all, who would care about me? The marriage was really over then. It just took a few more years for me to get that it was over. God, knows I tried. I used to write him letters, I kept being *Suzie Homemaker*. One time I even wrote an essay on how much I loved him and what a perfect life I had, and how lucky I was to have this blissful life. I guess I thought that if I wrote it and said it, maybe the storybook marriage fairy would drop out of the sky, wave a sparkly wand and we would drift off into the sunset in a cloud of fairy dust.

But all of us who have ever been there know that no matter how clean the house is, how well cared for the family is, how many loaves of bread, brownie batches, bake sale pies and cakes, they do not make a marriage. Two people make a marriage. Not a giver and a taker. Of course, life came up and smacked me square up-side my head. Again.

Sometimes I wish I could go on a lecture circuit and save women from themselves. Because that is what it is. We fool ourselves into believing that we can fix what is broken and most often the sad truth is that the possibility of a nurturing relationship never even existed in the first place. Trying to fix our marriage was like putting a tourniquet on the wind.

But over the years when I have had to morn this marriage and wonder when it really died, that was the time where there no possibility of putting Humpty Dumpty back together again. I kept gluing the pieces back together, but the cracks and the missing pieces just kept getting bigger. We convince ourselves that there is something we can do to fix the broken and missing parts.

Birthdays have a way of making us think about the past and the future. We all have our ghosts. Mine raise their angry heads and rattle more than I would like. But as time passes and the good outweighs the bad, I am able to see how lucky I am now.

There are so many good marriages. I have friends who have it all. I have tried so hard to understand what makes the difference. One thing is very clear to me. The couples that like each other, respect each other and enjoy each other make a go of it.

What we really do not know when we are young and in the throws of physical love, is that the extreme physical love part does not last unless you have the real deal. I just did not get that either time out. I got the intense *"Can't wait to get you into bed"* part. I just did not get the *"Wow, you are really fun to be with and I love doing things with you"* part.

Mora came into the dinning room carrying serving spoons and a huge bowl of French Vanilla ice-cream.

She looked at me and said, "Hey, Glory Girl, you OK? You look so sad. This is not a sad time. Lex is fine. She has been joking and laughing all evening."

I put on my happy face, and said to Mora, "Hey, it was about me, I was just having a mini pity party. I'm fine now." She gabbed me as I walked past her and we did the hug that friends do when they really care. Sometimes that all I need.

I added the two flower arrangements that matched the cake colors of red, white, silver and black. Not easy to find, I might add. I had found silver colored mats and nap-kins. Candle light, crystal, silver. Beautiful. The fire crackled and shot a soft warm glow into every corner of the room. The deep stone fireplace that opened to both the living and dining room gave the room and the evening an old world feel. The stones in the massive fireplace had been quarried right out of Haverstraw over a hundred years ago. The deeply etched colors run from obsidian black to an icy white and every hue in between. I marvel at their beauty every time I start a fire. I wonder about the men who dug them out the solid rock that held the secrets of our earth since its inception. And I wondered about the men who had created this viscerally beautiful wall that no artificial, man-made material could ever come close to matching.

We could have been a group of friends from any time in the last century. I could hear their gentle voices and the silvered laughter. These women are my muses. We are lucky if we have one good friend. I have five. It just doesn't get any better than that.

Mora and I continued setting out the crystal desert plates, placed the good silver and we pronounced it perfect. After everything was lit, I turned down the overhead chandelier and Mora went to the living room and invited the birthday girl and everybody to join us.

Lex came in first and stopped at the doorway. The soft light reflected her tears as she looked at the table starring her cake. She crossed to me and grabbed me in a bear hug, "I guess I had better stop whining about being alone." That brought on hugs all around. After a chunk of emotional overload, we all took our usual places and waited for Lex to cut her cake.

Lex began examining each character on the cake. "How do I cut into this? It is a work of art!"

Reg piped up, "Oh, just cut the damn thing! You can set the figures off to the side. And if I know Glory, she has already taken a shit-load of pictures. Right? Oh, Picture Taker of Everything!"

Lex, true to form, took her time removing the figures. I knew she would freeze them and they would find there way to other cakes and other occasions.

She finally began cutting the cake and began passing out the very generous slices.

For a few minutes, all was very quiet. I told everyone that there would be enough for each to take home another slice and Lex would have a large hunk to take home and continue *her day*. I had the bakery give me some pretty silver-colored, take-home boxes.

"OK, ladies, what is your pleasure? What's the next story of the evening? Do we want to sit in here or do we want to go back to the living room?"

Georgie stood up, "I think the living room is good but what about a potty break and then a walk around your luscious seawall walkway ? I am stiff as a cob."

The group affirmed this as a great idea. Everybody dispersed to my three bathrooms.

As soon as all were assembled in the kitchen, we trooped outside into the cool air. We walked down the cobbled walkway that had been placed there by long-ago-hands and followed it to the rockwall that had been erected over a hundred years ago. Sometimes I felt as old as the wall.

The moon shot a silver ribbon across the Hudson River and I was reminded why I live here. Lex and I shared a look that said she was thinking the same thing. We spend much of our together-time in this spot.

I have told Lex about my past and situations that I have endured in my marriages. I have been married twice, and had as many divorces. After the second failed, I finished raising my children and immersed myself in my teaching career.

I have published two books. The first one is *The Correlation of Shakespeare's Life and the Tragedies*, the second one is *The Liberation of George Eliot*. Lex has written two books on Joyce. *Joyce, Portrait and Parnell*, her second book is coming out this spring, *Charles and Katherine, Love in Bloom.*

We are collaborating on a book about Joyce's rejections of old world ideas politically, religiously, culturally and literary structures. We have already done almost four years of research on it. Dublin is our favorite city for both research and for fun. It is a labor of love and great experiences in Ireland. We are both dotty over anything Irish and most specifically about Joyce.

Occasionally when we are in a fed up mood with issues in our lives, we fantasize about moving to Ireland. Makes for fun *pie-in-the-sky* talk because we both know we have too many ties here to ever leave. But it does make for a great de-stressor.

We spend a month in Ireland every summer. Lucky for us and for the group, we all share dog sitting. When we go as a group we have a Bambi (I kid you not, that is her real name!) comes and stays at my house and she takes care of the entire pack. The dogs all get along as well as we do. Bambi is a nursing student who is dog sitter, dog trainer and all-things wonderful to us because we can go off on our little trips and not worry about our canine companions.

Lex and I are both deeply mired into The Irish experience and especially how influential both Joyce and Parnell were. We spend countless hours discussing every aspect of *Home Rule,* how Ireland changed because of these two and we spend wonderful hours discussing the incredible love story between Parnell and Katherine. We dig for each little scrap of information about Joyce and the history of his time period.

I know Lex is working on a fiction novel but I have never read any of it. Even as BFFs, there is a well of reserve about her and I know that much of her past is very painful.

With kind of an unspoken agreement, we walked without talking except for mundane generalities about the night, the landscaping and how beautiful everything is. We all love living near the Hudson River. All six of us live either by the River or within walking distance of it.

I have a set of Adirondack chairs that I bought many years ago on a vacation out to Montauk that are under an old grape arbor by the seawall. I asked if anybody wanted to sit. JJ and Reg did. The arbor is covered with both grape vines and honeysuckle. A gentle breeze was wafting heavenly smells in our direction as well as enveloping the sitters. The rest rambled further down the seawall.

2:-06 AM

Fresh air and our half hour trek around the property seemed to revive all of us. I said, "Hey, my Homies, I am ready to go in and I am eager to hear the next story."

Back inside everybody got really comfy with pillows and draped themselves on the chairs and couches. I kind of scooched and moved my backside until I was comfortable in my chaise. I pronounced that I would not stand for my story because it was going to be epic. As the grand old dame of the group I deserved to sit.

Several of the group looked surprised because they know how private I usually am, suddenly everything became quiet. I was struck with how much love and caring existed in this group of middle-aged women. Collectively, we have been through so much and we have all arrived where we are by being not only survivors, but women who change the world. Not being really melodramatic here. We do. We teach. We pass on a passion of knowledge of the world for that next generation and along the way, we do change the lives of those we interact with.

So maybe now was the time for me to share a little more of myself with those I care about the most other than my own children. I began,

> You know, I hardly know where to begin. I made a mistake a long time ago and talked about some of the things I have endured. I was very bitter for a long time. It came back and bit me in the butt.

But then, I don't think that not talking about it has been much better. There was a very long stretch where I had lost the bitterness. It was really to the point where I went for years without even thinking about Col. But then he would do something that stirred the pot and it was the same old hurt all over again. Now, all these years later, this man has managed to outdo anything he had ever done before. Something that I would not even have expected from him. And he has found a new way to abuse me by using the now grown children. Sadly, they are caught up in the drama of it all and do not realize they are being used. They are just collateral damage in his playbook. And I guess ego boosters. Sometime things in life are just a no-win situation. I also think that humans have a tendency to shape what the facts are into what they want to believe. We are all colored and shaped by our previous experiences.

Research is just beginning to tap into how much childhood experience is imprinted on the adult self and few people escape that early influence. There I go! My analytical side at war with my human side. Give me a platform and I am off and running. Back to my story.

Sorry, I will try not to go off on tangents. Lex, before you say anything, I know, I have a tendency to digress!

Are you guys sure that you want to hear this? There is a doo-doo load. It'll take a while. What is your pleasure, Ladies?

"Please go on." Georgie said, "You know this is a sisterhood. Not to be drippy, but this is how we all get rid of some of the pain. We all just have different stories that got all of us to the same place. I just read an article about carrying this kind of baggage. The psychiatrist said that people should not be concerned with moving on but with moving ahead, and that is exactly what we are doing. These sharings are such a part of that process. Babe, remember, there is a lotta love in this room."

I gave everybody a grateful look and launched into my saga.

You asked for it. Tell me when you need a break. This is probably a two-parter, maybe even three!

You already know I was raised in New Mexico. My parents were both artists who specialized in Indian paintings. They eventually owned shops in several cities. They never gained much respect as artists, but they became known as having an eye for discovering talent in other artists. They have done quite well over the years.

They have a great marriage. What they don't have is much interest in me or my sister Viv. We each made our own world at school.

So my sister and I learned how to create our own little world. We had each other and we both loved school. We were into everything, activities, sports, school government. So we were big fishes in our own little microcosmic part of the world of school.

Fortunately I was also a voracious reader and a secret writer. Writing has always been my way of dealing with my world. I had never shown anybody what I had written not even Viv. At least not until I started applying for scholarships and colleges.

I have always been a diary keeper so I used it as a resource and turned it into a book about school life. And fortunately for me, when I finally showed it to my English teacher when I was a junior, it was a stepping stone to a scholarship.

I didn't know if I wanted to go into law or literature but over time I kept leaning toward teaching.   I guess I forgot to research the difference of earning power.

Long story short, I got myself a full ride to Princeton. I got a job in a bookstore with a great boss who accommodated my school hours and I did my time and walked out with a B.A. and teacher's certification.

Fortunately, Viv came had come east with me and I was able to help her get through Penn State.

My plan had been to apply for a teaching position and to that end I was sending out applications all over The Tri-State area. Somebody told me about Hudson River College. I applied. Got it.   I have had offers over the years to bigger schools but I have never had the desire to leave the school or the area. It has been a good fit for me. Being head of our English Department has been where I think I excel and make the best contribution I can make. Cop out? I don't know, but I know I am very happy with what I have achieved professionally.

But sadly, success and achievement have been totally elusive for me in my private life. My social success has been only in academia and in my wonderful connection to Lex and to our group. I have not had success in mates. Well, that has been pretty obvious to even the most casual observer, has it not?

Some of you may think that I met Collier through school. I didn't. He was a plumber.

Mora interrupted, "And you let that go? What were you thinking?" The group laughed and I sighed, and answered, "Well, maybe I wouldn't have if had only been working on my pipes." This brought on a fit of giggles from JJ and vehement *Amens* from the others.

I continued.

Bought my first cute little cottage in Haverstraw, right on our mighty Hudson River. Adorable place but all kinds of needed repairs, especially bad plumbing. Col shows up, buff, funny, charming and the upshot was that I fell *in love*. Head over heels, just like the goopy, loopy stories in every romance novel. My prince with a wrench and a beat up van. Yep, *I was in love*. I am the walking, talking poster girl for love is blind. It is also deaf and dumb.

I never had a serious relationship before. Oh, yeah, casual boyfriends in school but they just never stuck. I never had those feelings that all of the other girls were chattering endlessly about. I couldn't see what the big deal was. The idea of hopping into bed or worse, climbing over the back seat with one of the lotharios was abhorrent to me. Ugh. Viv and I were popular, we did all the right stuff. I think we were pursued because we were both "un-getable". Same thing for college.

I was the nut-ball that would rather read a good book on Saturday night than go out clubbing. And to make it worse and cement my total *geekyness*, I didn't drink, didn't smoke and I sure as Hell, didn't do drugs. Didn't even want to hang out with anybody who did. Not surprising, I wound up getting a single dorm room. But, hitting the books instead of bars did wonders for my grades. Graduated in the top 10.

Viv met her husband after college too. She met him at a party given by the law firm where she was working. She had started law school and was working part time. She married a year later and never went back to school.

But I never got that *icy thrill in the pit of my stomach* or any of the other ooey, gooey feelings. I just thought I was different and I would marry someday when it was appropriate. I knew that I wanted children and that seemed to be what I would have to do to get to the children part.

JJ, laughed, and said, "That is so you, Glory. You over-think everything. Mind over matter! Then your "matter" got you in the end. Ha! No pun intended." This got the group going, so I waited out the gross comments and laughter. JJ hiccupped out, "Sorry, I was just imagining you in that dopy state. It does not compute. *Please to continue, Oh-Wise-One.*"

Well, I was not so wise this time. I was a total goner in days. All out, smitten, bitten, in a full blown infatuation that I thought was love. So this is what it was like! I am playing all the love songs on my eight-track, reading the Bard's sonnets, reading both Brownings, and more.

Do you guys see a pattern here? We are all high achievers, we all had such plans, we all got waylaid by nature. Don't tell me that gender isn't destiny. We are no different from our cave sisters. We just dress a little better.

Back to my saga, I was shouting from the roof tops, even my students were commenting that I seemed different. I came close to breaking into song in the classroom.

Calm, cool, analytical, realist me, was convinced that this was my destiny. My new life, I did not slow down one whit, full steam ahead.

Called my folks and told them that I was going to get married and hoped they could come to New York for the ceremony. This news was met with their usual disinterest disguised as, 'Business just will not permit us to leave right now,' so I accepted that I would be doing this on my own except for Viv and a few friends.

You know the park area between Nyack and Piermont down by the river? Somehow that seemed to be a romantic spot and since I did not belong to a church or any formal group of any kind, a good place to have this wonderful union that would last a lifetime.

"Hey, anybody seeing any thing wrong with the plan yet?" I gave a rueful laugh and plunged on.

The problems started exactly three months after our little water's edge union. Three months!

I don't think Col and I ever sat down and had an actual conversation that involved the real world. We did not know anything about each other. When we did start learning, it was too late.

You know, I wish we would give classes in high school about the concept of physical attraction. How many females mistake a physical response about *"being in love"*. Oh, I know, try telling a young girl anything. It is really clear now, but not then. And I did not even have the excuse of being that young!

Viv really did not like Col. She had his number right away. She kept telling me that I was rushing it and I did not know him well enough to make this huge decision. But look, I was already in my mid twenties. I would like to think that if I had understood nature better I would have known that just because my body was responding, it did not mean I could build a relationship that would be there for the long haul.

Clear case of nature vs. brains. I think the brain goes dormant when the love bug bites. Wonder what our wonderful esteemed Bio Department instructors would think about my theories. Betcha they have the same ideas, they just explain it better!

But then I look at the kids today and I think that we can't tell them anything either. Do they listen to our experiences and say, 'Oh, yes, tell us OH-WISE-ONES, and we will listen and not make the stupid mistakes that you have made?' Nope.

Look at the literature we teach. Hundreds of years of *Boy Meets Girl* and then the problems begin. Lack of communication is always at the top of the list. Two by two, we jump in before we know what the other person is all about and then wonder why we have problems after the "glow" wears off.

Notice my word glow! Boy did I clean that up. See, no F bomb! But each and every one of us knows exactly what I mean. I think it's a crap shoot. Some of us get that wonderful guy and off we go to the suburbs to be immersed into wedded bliss. We live happily ever after with somebody who loves us, nurtures us, and fulfills all the other needs that we have. Some get the lollypop and some just get the stick. I got two sticks. And if truth be told, maybe I am a stick too. I don't know at this point.

Why do we believe that "love" will take care of everything? When the reality is that what we mistake for love is often just lust. Jimmy Carter was right or at least his concept is. The problem is that all too often we act on the idea of lust instead of waiting to see if it is love.

You know, I could pontificate for hours on what the Hell LOVE is. I have read myself silly trying to understand what it is and I don't think I know any more that when I started. As close as I can come is that pure love is what we have in this room. Yes Group, I know, I am off topic again.

OK, OK, I will stop waxing philosophical. Back to my sad, and oh, so Damn common tale.

We were so polarized that Col and I could have been different species. We did not even speak on any topic that had interest for the other. I would talk about classes, students or any of my passions and his eyes would glaze over. In the beginning I would try to engage Col by asking him about his work but I was just as guilty as he was because I could not work up any enthusiasm about the plumbing job he would be doing. Over time, and not really that much time, we just stopped talking except for the day to day minutia. Bills, work on the house, car issues and the other day to day talk. Sadly, I think this is a lot more common than society wants to acknowledge.

Col never talked about any of his jobs. When he was home, which became more and more infrequent, he just either be out in the garage tinkering with something, usually an old car he would be working on, or he sat in front of the TV and even after the kids came he just barked at the kids and me it if we were foolish enough to try to talk to him. Even during commercials, we learned to leave him alone. But I will have to say that we always had the cleanest garage and storage area. He even had a little black and white TV and a big La-Z-boy in it. Over time he spent more and more time out there.

He started coming home later. The excuses were that the job took longer than expected. Then he was staying out even later, coming in buzzed. Then into the wee hours, drunk.

Within a couple of years it had gone from those very brief, love-charged days to being verbally berated, slapped, shoved, and constantly being told that I had no value. Those first five years were a living Hell for me except for the birth of my children.

I was living in three different worlds. My children, my teaching and my life with Col. The main part of my life, was being a mother to those wonderful children. Every ounce of energy was focused on them. No need to talk about the Boy Scouts, Girl Scouts, bake sales, school activities. We have all done it all. When I look back on this time, I realize that for the most part, the kids and I were happy. I worked very hard at making things as normal as possible. And I loved every minute of their childhood. I reveled in it.

But there were the three distinct parts to my life. School was wonderful. That made me one of the lucky ones. I have always thought about the women who had nothing. No job or career and some with no children. So while two of the parts of my life, shored me up and gave me purpose the third was the part that would not let life become *Ozzie & Harriet*.

Every time Col did something such as staying out all night or smacking me if I displeased him, he told me that it was my fault. Sadly, I think I began to accept this. How in the world does this work? I knew I was a good teacher, knew I had value in my academic world, knew I was a good parent. Nobody ever loved their kids more, and I did what I had to do to provide for their happiness in every way.

So why did I accept his opinion of who I was. I don't know how or why, but I compartmentalized these worlds. He never criticized my parenting. But he focused on what a horrible wife I was. I had even less value as a bed partner. And I bought into this. Hook, line and sinker. And since I was a virgin when I got married, I had no other data to compare. Yes, Group, I was the world's oldest virgin.

Yes, intellectually, I do know that it is the Stockholm Syndrome. It is such a simple idea, that it seems like it is an easy explanation. It was long after I was away from Col before I understood it. If somebody had told me before I married, I would wind up in that kind of relationship, I would been insulted and rejected the idea completely. Not me. I was woman, hear me roar. Well, at home I wasn't roaring.

He was now staying away for days at a clip. It became common for him to stay away for two or three days, no phone call, nothing. I didn't argue about it because the reality was that it was easier than dealing with him at home. I'm not saying that it didn't hurt. It was a constant rejection.

Given a choice, I wanted that warm and fuzzy husband and father. Not what I got. And no matter how hard I tried, nothing changed.

Thank God, for teaching. Or I would have been one of the barefoot and pregnant set. Col had no problem with my paycheck coming in.

It became common for me to have to call on friends for transportation to school. After a while I didn't even make excuses about it, I would call and ask for a ride. My rides would check with me at the end of my classes to see if I needed a ride home. I usually did.

One time I was foolish enough to suggest to Col that we might want to invest in a second car. He snapped, 'Why, so you can show off to all your stuck-up, educated, hoity-toity, friends?' I didn't suggest it again.

One Friday he came in about four in the afternoon, showered and came out into the bedroom to dress.

I asked him if he were going out and he said that it was none of my business. I told him that if he were going to be gone very long, I would need to go to the store because I was out of grocery items that I would need for the kids. Since he was driving my car, our only car, I would need to use the car. I started over to his dresser to get the keys, and before I could reach for them, he backhanded me and knocked me off my feet.

I was as shocked as I was hurt. It was one thing to have him slap or shove but quite another to have been punched. He was immediately apologetic and the "*it will never happen again*" lies began. I used the car, got what I needed and as soon as I was back, he was off. Gone for the week end. So much for the apology. But as usual, I wanted to believe that the punch could not happen again.

Of course it happened again. And again. I made excuses to myself. I made excuses to the doctors when I did go for medical help. And of course the doctors were all too happy to accept these excuses when it was clear that there was something else going on.

One of they typical "*bad times*" occurred on one of the rare occasions where we had taken the kids to the zoo.

Col had put a six-pack into the trunk and he went out to the car frequently. It was clear that he was grabbing and downing a beer on each of these little side trips. By the time we left the zoo and returned to the car, the six-pack was finished and he was in no shape to drive. But that did not stop him from driving.

Col was speeding and driving erratically. I asked him to slow down. He glared at me and drove faster. He turned on the radio and was blasting it. I foolishly reached over and turned it down. His right arm shot out and backhanded me. His heavy, class ring caught me right under my left eye.

Just a few miles from home, the flashing red lights from a police car pulled us over. After the cop had written the ticket, he leaned in and saw that my eye was bleeding and swelling. He asked what happened. Col quickly told him that we had been to the zoo and I had slipped and fallen against a post and that is why he was speeding to get me to the emergency room at the hospital by our house so that I could get medical care for the injury.

The cop did not ask one me a Damn thing directly. Not about my eye or try to see if Col had been drinking, which should have been very clear to any observer. I, of course, did not say a word.

We *say* that we are a country that takes care of our people. Especially women and children. Well, we pay lip service to the problems of abuse.

Nobody gets it unless you are really in the situation. I tried to get help, I really did. What I got was a lot of questions about 'What did I do to cause it?' or 'Why did I stay if the abuse was so bad?' Sadly over time we begin to believe that we do cause the problems and deserve the abuse.

How we hide what is happening to us. It was years before I even told Viv. I am sure she knew, but she also knew I just wasn't ready to talk about it and I was not ready to acknowledge that I had a failed relationship.

I was so ashamed. Somehow, I saw it as my failure. If I were better, or different, he would not be doing this. Even before I told Viv about the physical abuse, she tried for years to tell me that it was not my fault and I had to get out. Viv would tell me that I was becoming less of a person. So who did I get angry with? Viv, of course. She pushed but she was afraid to push too hard. Now I realize that we don't listen until we are ready to, even to the point of pushing away the people who are trying to help.

It took a long time. I guess I was very fortunate in that I left before there was nothing left of me to be a person. Even as close as the six of us are, you would not have known there was another Glory at home if you had known me then. We hide it so well. Some of us are able to lose that other person, and some become it. I have known so many women that never got back to being a full person. They were always afraid, thought of themselves as failures and were never able to fit the pieces back together.

What is even more astonishing to me is that the abuser has the ability to appear to be such a "good guy" to the outside world. I have a natural outgoing, excitable nature. You guys, just like the rest of the world, see the person I am. Back then, everybody at school saw the teacher.

Nobody knew about the quiet, scared, apprehensive person at home. As is the case with so many abused women, neighbors and friends would not have believed me if I told them about the abuse. From the outside, I appeared to be the volatile one.

One of the things I have learned is never to judge a relationship. What the outside sees is not necessarily what really going on from the inside. Every person who is in a relationship knows that what the outside world sees is not really what is going on inside. And yet people will make judgments based only what they see. Even some who have been abused themselves. That is the part I have never understood. Why will somebody think that they can judge a relationship unless they lived every part of it? The abuser and the abused hide the actual actions for obvious reasons. The abuser knows he does not want to be judged for these actions and the abused is ashamed and has become to believe they are somehow partially responsible for what is happening to them. Sad.

I'll tell you one other crazy thing. I know women who have been abused themselves, either verbally, physically or both. And they have said to me, 'Oh, but you are so strong', or insert whatever word here you want, 'You would have left if it had been that bad.' That is how bad the misconceptions are. The general public just does not see that a strong person can get beaten down both physically and mentally. And even some who have been abused do not believe others. Terrorism works.

I just recently read a book by a psychologist who said that abuse is terrorism. Abuse has an objective by the abuser. It takes many forms but the bottom line is control and punishment. Often the abuser is trying to rid himself of childhood demons.

Some of his research results particularly fascinated me. He named Type One, The Cyclic Abuser. He described them as having a) growing patterns of escalating tension, violent out bursts and periods of denial or atonement b) sees the victim as simultaneously engulfing them and abandoning them c) seeks emotional intimacy and at the same time fears it. D) can be described as being two distinct people, the one that is presented to the public, usually charming and sometimes even Happy-Go-Lucky, and the one that the abuser presents to the victim(s) e) holds the victim as being responsible for what actions he takes toward the victim.

Fortunately for me, the more I read and learn about abuse, the less responsibility I take for what was done to me. At a meeting of victims that I attended for several years, one of the most common comments was 'You know, I never, ever thought this could happen to me. I was too secure, too strong, too sure of myself. But there I was, a victim for years. I think it sneaks up on us.' One of the most common things that we all shared with each other was that we all had harbored hope for years that things would change.

One time I tried to report it. It had been just one time too many. Col had come home drunk, got into bed and tried to roll me over into *position*. On those rare occasions I had always been very submissive. That night I wasn't. Col turned over and I huddled against the edge of the bed. I felt him moving around and thought he was trying to get comfortable and go to sleep. Wrong! He had been getting into position to kick me square in my back. I flew off the bed, and because I had a drawer open on the bedside table, I had three direct hits when I landed. My head on the top of the bedside table, my shoulder on the open drawer and my hip on the tile floor. That was in addition to the kick to the middle of my back. I looked like a sacked quarter back after a Jets game.

I went to the local Police Department. Well, just my luck, several of the cops knew Col. One of them took the report. Everything in his body language told me that I was not being believed. I finished my report of the event and the cop looked at me and with a perfectly straight face, asked me if there were any witnesses.

I repeated that it had happened in the middle of the night, in the bedroom. Who did he think was a witness? He asked, 'Well, what about your kids? They would have heard something like this wouldn't they?' Then he said he would have to interview them. I said that was impossible.

Col was always very careful in front of the kids or anybody else. As this was coming out of my mouth, I realized how foolish I sounded. And here again, I was the one that was made out to be the liar, the wrong one, and the one trying to sully the good guy. Since his outward persona was that of Mr. Good Guy, Mr. Fun-Time-Drinking-Buddy and he was never verbally or physically abusive in public, then this just had to be made up didn't it?

By now, I was on the verge of hysteria, further cementing the cop's opinion of me. I asked him if I could show the bruises to a woman cop. He said, 'Sure, but bruises alone do not prove how a person got them.'

Well, it was pretty clear that I was not going to get any where with reporting what had happened. All I had done was make my situation worse at home. Much worse.

A raging Col came home that night. It had not taken long for his buddies to report my reporting. Of course, he waited for the kids to go to bed. How smart he was. Is, I guess. Anyway, nobody ever saw what he was doing. That night was the same old story.

Viv was the one who certainly connected the bruises to where they came from. The rest of my world was blissfully unaware.

One time, one of my students came into my classroom before class, and as he handed me his assignment said, 'Mrs. Gaston, how many doors can you run into?' And he gave me a very long look. After class he waited for the room to empty, came up to my desk, and said, 'My mom, ran into a lotta doors too. She is divorced now and she is very happy.' Then he reached over and patted me on the shoulder. He left the room and I dissolved into tears.

Nobody gets what is going on unless they have lived it and this kid had *lived it* with his mother. For the rest of that semester, he used to leave me little notes of encouragement and candy bars. One time he left me a beautiful Gunn Bear. I still have it. So, I am off on another tangent, Back to the story.

When Col was at home I became more and more Little-Miss-Mousey. I was in constant fear of what I would do or say that might set off the next round of abuse.

Look at us. There are two of us in our group with similar experiences. Since I got involved with working with groups that are trying to educate and help young girls, I have been doing research about it. And the stats are staggering.

Oh, my God, I hate being a statistic, a cliché, another victim. And I hate all of the questions I have had to endure. And all these years later, women are still being asked the same damn questions.

'Why didn't you just leave?'

'Why didn't you tell anybody?'

'Why did you lie about all of the black eyes and worse? Doesn't that make you a liar?' Well, of course, it does. But telling the truth didn't work either. So there is even added guilt because we are lying to so many people. Especially those we care about. Just one big vicious circle.

There are many reasons why women stay. But most of them are surprisingly the same. I have spent a lot of time trying to find out myself.

The worst one of the questions? Because it is really more of a statement to us rather than a real question. 'Oh, you are such a strong person, I can't imagine you putting up with anything.' So there is the not so implied statement. It is flat out an observation on the commenter's disbelief of my sad little story. I must be exaggerating or worse lying. Here's the deal about that. Who the Hell lies about being abused? It is humiliating.

An ego buster. Because even in our own heads, we have to be the guilty ones. I still have vestiges of believing I did something wrong. I didn't measures up or it wouldn't have happened to me.

I just read another article recently about how many women who have been living this double life, tried to get out and were killed in the process. Does not matter if the person being abused is weak or strong. So, I guess I count myself among the lucky ones. Col, at least, was not one of those.

Society really does a number on those who are abused. How long will it be before we take the stigma off the abused and put it where it should be? Every damn time I think I have put it behind me something happens and I get that same *sick-to-my-stomach-feeling*. I do it every time I get evaluated if it is a male evaluator. If it is a woman, I just sail through it.

But the really sad thing is that abused women stay in these relationships for all the wrong reasons. The worst part? Some who are able to walk away already have their essence killed.

Look how many who are abused are really trapped. And when they do try to break away, the abuser either stalks them, or hurts them, or kills them.

One of the reasons we stay is because we want to believe the person we love will not do it again. When they tell us the lies, we believe because if we do not, everything in our life is a lie.

In my case, the beginning of my nightmare came at the same time that I found out that I was pregnant. It is not an excuse, just a fact, like many abused women, I did not have a safety net. I knew my parents were not going to welcome me and an baby with open arms.

I focused everything on the coming baby. Col was staying out more and more but in a way, I found that easier. He was becoming more verbally abusive. Everything was my fault. He didn't want to stay home because I was unattractive to him. The names got worse. It was a steady barrage of how I did not measure up.

I know, how stupid could I have been? Really! Of course it is so easy to see now. But it is not so easy to see when you are in it.

The larger part of my life became getting ready for this new creature, this new love, this new life that until I felt that first flutter of life, I never realized I wanted that new life more than anything. Even before she was born, I was in real love. This life forming within my being, her heart beating below mine became everything.

I was compartmentalizing. Yep, so easy to see now.

Col became almost a ghost in my life. When he was home, I could almost tune out the steady stream of why he was justified in his drinking, his staying away, he lack of feelings for me or this child I was carrying.

I learned how to tip-toe around him. I fixed the meals, kept the little house spotless, washed, ironed, sewed, mended, made curtains out of sheets, never spent any money, including mine, turned over my paychecks, and went out to teach my classes everyday.

I was really living two different lives. No, really three. A mother who wanted to be the best mother possible, competent, confident teacher, and abused wife.

At school I was fearless, competent, funny, a self-starter, and I was respected by both faculty and students. I am certain, if I had told faculty or students about my home life, they would have been convinced that I was joking or delusional.

One experience during that time, hurts me to this day. I had been able to convince Col to go to a Christmas Faculty Party because he liked the idea of the free booze. We were seated at a table of ten. Professor Bendig and his wife Molly were seated directly across from Col and me. We were in public so I was laughing and having a good time.

Col always cultivated his good guy persona in public and it was one of the times that I felt safe to act like my real self around him.

Col's public image was very important to him. I think he needed it too, because somehow that helped to validate his own sense of his image as Mr. Goody-Two-Shoes.

Col had made several trips to the open bar and I was beginning to be concerned about his behavior which could change in an instant when he was drinking. At one point he leaned over and asked me how much longer he would be stuck at this stupid dinner. After all, free booze at the open bar beckoned him. I answered as quietly as I could that it would be a little longer because there were going to be a couple of speeches. Col hissed back that he was not there to listen to any boring teachers ramble on about stupid, boring stuff.

Unfortunately, he was loud enough to be heard by everyone at the table. I tried to whisper back that it would only take a little while. Col flashed back, loudly this time, 'Don't tell me to be patient or I am outta here.' And with that he lurched up and left the table. I did not know if he were going to the bar or home and for once I didn't really give a Damn where he was going. But I was mortified about his behavior at the table.

Molly gave me a long look, nodded her head just slightly. I am sure that I was the only one who saw either the look or the tiny nod. That exchange spoke volumes. In that instant, I knew that we shared an abysmal experience. We looked at each other and exchanged a common bond. We acknowledged sympathy and understanding that nobody who has not experienced this kind of abuse can ever know. I have thought about that tiny nod for more years than I want to count.

I have always been sorry that I did not seek her out to become a friend. I don't even know why I didn't. It is one of my great regrets in that life-bag of regrets.

Some of you know the end of this story. Less than two years later, Mr. Good guy, the well respected Professor Bendig beat Molly to death. Maybe if I had become her friend, we might have both gotten out sooner and she might still be alive to be a mother to her children. They lost both their mother and father. She is gone because a man thought he had the right to abuse his wife.

Before it happened, nobody knew what she had endured. Nobody thought he was capable of doing this. Outwardly, he was the perfect husband and the perfect father. The children never had a clue either. He had never abused any of the four children.

Molly's autopsy told a very different story than what had been presented by the image he earned outside of those closed doors. Her body told the story of what she had endured over the years.

I know most people think that these things can't go together, but millions of women are walking this tightrope every day. Competent, achieving, wonderful women. Even a few men. Five percent of the abusers are female. There are so many hidden stories of women, children and even a few men who are abused and hiding it from public view. We are ashamed. We somehow begin to believe the abuser and that we have done something to deserve what we get.

I know, I am circling all over the map here. But this topic is so painful, and so close to my inner core, I get nuts every time I talk about it. Over the past few years, I have not talked about it much. I just read about it, trying to understand more and I work as a volunteer for a shelter to do what I can to help.

So, back to just before Mia was born.

Lucky for me I was due July 2nd. So I would not need to have time off and I would be able to go back to work at the beginning of the new semester. Little did I know how hard that was going to be. To have to walk out that door every morning leaving my precious baby in somebody else's care.

Keeping my eyes on the prize, life went on. Col did not hit me again until a couple of months later. He had made a coffee table out of scrap wood and put tile on the top. A piece of tile pulled up and I asked him one Saturday if he could fix it.

Surprisingly, he said 'Sure,' and took the table out to the carport, got his tools and began to work. He called me to come out to hold the table while he tried to put the tile into place. I was holding onto the end of the table the best that I could as his strength was pushing against me. He kept yelling, 'Hold the damn table like I am telling you!' Finally, the table slipped, and shot out away from me. His fist came up and smashed the table, came up again and knocked me flat with a shot to my jaw. Lucky for me my jaw was not broken, just cracked. And the story I told the Doctor? Oh, My! I fell down the steps when I went outside to hang up clothes.

Well, let's see if I can cut to the chase. This went on for eleven years. Eleven years and two kids later, I was still part of this sad little saga and abuse cycle.

Maybe one of the women's magazines should have an article about abuse instead of *A Hundred Ways to Please Your Man in the Bedroom.* Maybe there should be a check list of behaviors to see if the reader is in a healthy relationship and a check list for what behaviors should be the signal for getting help.

I'll relate a few more of the instances. If I tried to tell everything we would be here until Lex's next birthday. By the way, I am fitting into another syndrome that is typical of abuse victims. We go for years keeping our mouths shut about what is happening to us. Most often nobody knows for years, they eventually a few people close to us suspect and then we are in denial and we make excuses. When we finally break away, suddenly we can't shut up about it. All that hurt and anger and our frustrations come bubbling out and suddenly we are Mt. Vesuvius.

After almost twelve years of bottling it up inside, not talking about it to anybody the dam broke. There had been a woman, a neighbor, who knew about the situation, during one serious event, I had fled to her house because I needed help. But I refused to go to the hospital. She had begged me to report it. And afterward, I would not talk about it with her. I avoided her after that.

But now the gates were open. It does not help me to know that this is a common syndrome, that once the victims start talking, it just keeps gushing out. I hate being part of this whole process. But I did talk, and talk and talk. Out came all of the frustration, the newly discovered anger and hurt. Most of all I was bitter.

For years, I did talk about it. Way too much. It really took me years to get that under control and know when to talk about it and when to just be quiet. So I think we get victimized again. When we talk about it most of the time other people do not want to hear about it. Usually they do not know what to do with the information and how to react to it.

I was always thinking up the next thing that would show Col what a good wife and good mother I was. I just knew that someday I would have the fairytale. Col would realize what a great life we could have and we would all live happily ever after. Obviously it had to be something that I was doing or something that I was not doing. I just knew that I had to keep working at getting it right.

Our anniversary was coming up. We had married during Thanksgiving week, so we used to celebrate the Saturday of that week every year. For some reason, Col seemed to like these anniversary parties. We would invite a few of my friends from school and quite a few of his drinking buddies. I was always on guard because I was always worried that he would drink to much and let his good-guy image slip but so far it had been in check for these yearly gatherings.

This was our eighth anniversary. Mia was six, and Biff was two. No school because of the holiday. I started cleaning and cooking early Friday. Friday afternoon, a couple of my friends offered to come help setup for the party. I had rented the "party house" in our development because our house was too small for that large a group. I always went all out. Decorations, lots of cooking and of course, drinks of choice.

Three of my teaching buddies who were on my cooking committee and I got back to the house just after dark. We had come back from decorating and were now going to spend the evening with me making all of the food for this shindig. I really looked forward to this party every year. Not just the party but the preparations that occupied me and my friends for weeks before the event.

Col was in the living room with several of his buddies, and they were all were drinking and watching something on TV. The lamps were off in the living room with only light coming from the flickering television set.

It was too early to put the kids to bed, so I had tried to keep them in the kitchen while we continued cooking even though I did not like the kids in the kitchen with all the confusion and preparations going on. But that seemed preferable to having them in the living room where the men were.

Suddenly, I realized that Biff was not in the kitchen and I walked into the living room just in time to see Biff reach up and grab a cigarette getting the business end right in the middle of his little palm. He screamed, I reached down, scooped him up, turned to Col and said, 'Put on some lights, it is not a teen party.' I would never have spoken this way normally. Unthinkable.

Biff getting burned had overridden common sense and self preservation. As soon as it flew out of my mouth, I realized that I was in for it. Of course, not while anybody was around. After all, Col had a good-guy reputation to uphold.

Col stood up, gave me a look that spoke volumes, and turned to his cronies, 'Hey, let's go to Sully's and let the women folk do what they find so all fired important.'

Woosh, they were off and I spent the next several hours with that icy fear in the pit of my stomach waiting for a very angry Col to get home and dreading what I knew was inevitable.

Just after four in the morning, Col came rolling in. He slammed into the bedroom and I tried to pretend to be asleep. He said, in that cold voice that he used when talking to me, 'Glory, I know you ain't asleep. Sit up when I am talking to you.' I did.

He looked me dead on and said, 'You know what? You ain't worth it. I'm going to sleep.' And he did. Life with Col was a constant emotional rollercoaster. I think that was worse than hitting me because it kept me off balance from knowing what would be next. I never did.

The next day was the party. I was physically and emotionally drained. I tried to talk to him several times during the hours before the party. No response. A couple of times, he told Mia to tell me something. He never spoke one word to me all day or at the party.

OK, I thought, he is doing his *not speaking to me* again. That was one of his "punishments".

This one exceeded his earlier accomplishments! He did not speak to me directly for over six months.

Do you have any idea how unnerving and horrible it is to live in a house with somebody who will not speak to you directly? No interaction. None. Fortunately this behavior sailed right over the kids heads.

Then one day he came home and had flowers and a box of candy. I wondered what was up. This had never been his way before. He would say he was sorry about something but then move on. Talk about being off balance. I just never knew what would be next. There seemed to no end to the surprises.

After I had put the kids to bed, Col asked me to come sit in the living room. Stranger and stranger. He was almost tearful. He told me that he had been to the doctor and he had been diagnosed with diabetes. That and heart disease run in his family. Anyway, he wanted to know if I would help by cooking the foods in his new diet plan.

He continued that was so sorry for the way he had treated me over the years. He was sure that it had to do with him being sick. He just knew that it was his sickness that made him behave the way that he did.

Well, I can tell you that many thoughts ran through my head, none of which I voiced out loud. If I knew nothing else, I knew when to keep my mouth shut when it had anything to do with Col.

Do I need to tell you that his newfound humility and needy demeanor lasted only a few months?

The worst was yet to come!

Col was from a big family in Clinton, NJ. They were only a short distance away, but we rarely ever saw them and he never made an effort to go there or have them come see us.

Col had an older sister whom I had met on the few occasions when we had gone to visit over the last few years. I found her to be absolutely wonderful. I did not meet Paula until a couple of years after I married Collin. As soon as we met, Paula and I had bonded. She had had her share of problems as well. She had commented one time that she wished we either lived closer or Col would make the effort to visit more.

One Saturday, right after he told me about his diabetes, he said, 'Get the kids ready, we are going to see Paula.'

So we bundled up the kids and drove to Clinton. It was even a pleasant drive. Col appeared to be in a good mood and was even joking with the kids. Now, I think it is sad to realize that only a few experiences stand out as being pleasant or good. For the most part, I do not think that the kids ever really understood the dynamics of their parent's relationship. Kids just accept what ever there is as normal. Of course, if they had been made aware of the physical abuse, instead of it being hidden from them, then they would have had an entirely different experience.

I have always been grateful that it was hidden from them. I know so many kids who had to be subjected to the abuse both to the mother and to themselves.

We arrived at Paula's and he asked her to talk with him. She was as surprised by his demeanor as I was. We settled all the kids in the living room with a video and then we sat down at Paula's kitchen table.

Over coffee and a sugar-free cake he told Paula about his medical situation and asked her a few questions about her same condition. She had been diabetic for years.

Then Col and Andy went outside to talk cars. Paula and I started chatting. I told her about his recent bout of not speaking. She told me that that was a trick that her father had done too. Then she started telling me the family history. None of which I had ever heard before.

Long story short, Yes, Ladies, this whole recitation could be longer! I am only briefly going to tell you what Paula told me about their childhood. There are parts of it that I do not even want to discuss. Their childhood had been a horrible one with the most problematic part being that Col had grown up being alternately abused and ignored. Paula, being older, had tried to do her best, but it had been a losing battle. Eight kids, alcoholic, abusive parents and the result is the man I married.

It made me realize that my childhood had been a walk in the park compared to his. His earlier, jovial mood seemed to have dissipated by the time we left.

Driving home, neither of us spoke, he in his thoughts and I in my newly found information and my sudden realization that it was never going to get better. Not a chance in Hell, that he would ever be more than exactly what he was. Much of his behavior was now clear. I realized that he really had not had a chance at knowing how to be a loving, nurturing husband. His father had been much worse than Col ever had been.

This newfound knowledge did not make things better for me. What it did, was tell me that everything I was hoping for, the great transformation, the great fairytale ending was just not going to happen ever. Not in a pig's eye.

But at the same time, I was still convinced that it was more important to stay because the children needed both parents. I was afraid to take their father away. I wanted two parents for them. And of course, I still managed to believe that the short flashes of the good Col outweighed the children not having him at all.

Col had never hurt the children physically. In public he was the jovial, gregarious, cut-up. The great, good-guy father. Put him in public or aim a camera at him and he was Dr. Jekyll. He had that part down pat. At home he was morose, nonverbal, distant and cold. To this day, I do not know why. Why did he choose to be unhappy when he was with me? And like all women who have experienced this, there is that self doubt that we carry for the rest of our lives. No matter how much evidence and conformation that we have value, there is still a part of us that doubts.

I was so conflicted. Intellectually, I knew things would never change. But there was still that tiny little part of me that kept hoping that the guy that came out it public might just take over and be that guy at home. The love I had for him at the beginning was eroding but there was still enough there for me to be hopeful. I was still young enough to be an optimist in the face of absolute proof.

I still did not think divorce. I knew what a I had. Still, I thought that that the kids needed two parents. The America Dream.   So we moved on. Nothing got better but still things were not any worse.   Amazing what the human spirit learns to endure.

The physical abuse became less but the verbal abuse was worse, My way of coping was that I tried to ignore and excuse. Well, he never had a roll model, he never learned love because he was never given love.   Ah, a new coping mechanism.

I began to spend my lunch-hours in the library trying to learn everything I could about abuse and childhood issues. It became very clear to me that we had been a collision course. Two very emotionally deprived people. We had each come into the marriage seeking a partner to help fill the lack that we each had. Instead we had each exacerbated the problem.

I needed unconditional love and a safe environment. One advantage that I had had was that my parents had loved each other. I am sure that in their own way, they loved Viv and me too. They just did not show it. But neither Viv or I had grown up with physical abuse or worse, psychological abuse.

Col had grown up without the modeling of how a parent should act or how a husband should behave. All he had ever learned was abuse.

All of you know Dr. Suzette Sanderson, the Head of the Psychology Dept. I sought her out during my quest for knowledge. I asked her if she could recommend somebody whom I could talk to.

Suzette was quiet for a minute, then said, 'How about me? I was a therapist in private practice before I started teaching.'

I had not known that. The upshot was that I started seeing her once a week for years. She wouldn't even let me pay her. She told me about an event in her life, and that somebody had counseled her and changed her life. I know she helped me cope. It was a slow process but she helped me see that I was not the problem and that

I did not deserve any of the abuse. She helped me see that even Col was not completely responsible for his behavior because of his own demons and what he endured as a kid.

Suzette had said that she would love to have him come in to see her too and that could be invaluable but we both agreed that the chances of that were nil. I was even afraid to tell Col that I was seeing her. I just told him I was teaching a class during the time that I saw her.

Suzette gave me sources to read and much of it explained many of the issues that Col and I had experienced. One of the behaviors I had not been able to understand was how he could be such a monster at home and yet present such a super-good-guy in public and even for the most part, in front of the kids. He had never hit me in front of them. And his verbal abuse was always so veiled that I knew what he was saying but for the most part it sailed right over the kids heads. As the kids got older he was even more careful. I was even grateful for this because it was a burden that I did not want them to share.

One session in particular stands out for me. Suzette shared with me that she has been doing research for a book on abuse. She said that she did not know if O.J. Simpson had killed his former wife, Nicole Brown Simpson and Ronald Goldman or not. Her gut told her that he had and all of the evidence seemed to point that way. But the real issue for her was what Nicole had endured before the murder as much as the murder itself.

'I do know that he did not deny beating her' Suzette continued. 'Women are beaten, stalked, terrorized by the men who profess to love them . There are so many graves of women who have been murdered by husbands, lovers, exes who feel they have a right to do this. How many millions are still behind doors suffering abuse and too terrorized to try to get away?'

'How many more victims have to be beaten, choked, throttled, bludgeoned, cut, stabbed, shot, cut, tortured, shamed, humiliated and treated as property before society finally allows women to become valued enough so that we teach both men and women that nobody has the right to devalue them. That is where the problem really is. Men grow up with a value system that prepares some to believe that this is not only acceptable but it is their right.'

'I had an interesting case shared with me not long ago that I have permission to use in my research. She was not my patient. Sadly she was not anybody's patient. Her husband was a policeman in Northern N.J. He had a girlfriend that he was so brazen about, he actually bought the girlfriend a house two blocks away from his wife and child because he did not want to have to drive that far when he left the house to go make a quick visit. The wife, I will call her Hanna, suspected that there was a girlfriend. She finally talked a cousin into following the lovely, two-timing husband. And lo and behold, the cousin finds out about the girlfriend and the little love nest.'

'Hanna, who has been brutalized both physically and mentally, arrives at the breaking point and she goes to a lawyer, and gets the husband removed. She had never reported any of the physical abuse but she had shared the incidences with her cousin and there were hospital records that matched up with what she had told the cousin.'

'The husband moves in with the girlfriend. This should have been the end of the story, right?'

'It wasn't. Husband is angry. The stalking begins. And he is not alone, his cop buddies join in. Police cars cruise up and down in front of her house, police cars follow behind her to and from work. Police in uniform show up in the grocery store, the library, where ever Hanna goes. And Hubby drags her into court for every thing he can trump up.'

'This goes on for two years. She tries to go to the police department for help. It just got worse.'

'She goes to work and little else. She is afraid to go out. Dating or having any kind of social life was impossible. She was afraid all the time.'

'One morning her car would not start and she called a friend to pick her up to take her to work. After work, another friend offered to drive her home. A male. She and the friend arrive home. A police car is in front. She rushes out of the car, and races inside of her house, to her safe place.'

'This did not turn out to be the case. Husband was inside and Hanna was beaten to death with his police baton. Her face was shattered beyond recognition and the autopsy revealed that most of her bones were broken. All this while the thirteen year old son was upstairs frantically calling the police, that for some reason, were particularly slow to respond to this event.'

'The husbands excuse was that she had embarrassed him in front of his cop buddies by kicking him out of HIS house for his little indigressions. And she had the audacity to get child support and part of his pension when she was the one who wanted the divorce. The worst part for me was that nobody on this police department seemed to think that he had been out of control or that his actions were a problem until after he killed her.'

'I think about that young boy often. How does he ever live a normal, trusting life? Another one of the casualties of abuse.'

'Another one of the cases that is being used by permission, in my research, has a first-hand account of the grown child who witnessed the murder of her mother at the hands of the father.'

We heard glass shatter, the sounds of a scuffle, furniture thumping and being moved. My brother ran from his room, jumped into my bed and held on tight to my shaking body. And then the sound of thump, thump, thump. My brother pushed me away and got off the bed, I followed. We got to the doorway of the kitchen where my father was slamming my mother against the cabinets. He had a handful of her hair and he was just slamming as hard as he could. Both my brother and I were screaming for him to stop. He didn't. There was so much blood. Everywhere. He was walking in it. We could smell the horrible, coppery, aroma that filled the air. I have never been able to get the sounds, the smell and the fear out of my head. And I have never been able to have a relationship with anybody because I do not trust anyone.

My father killed more than my mother that night. My brother committed suicide right after I graduated from high school. I guess he thought his job was done and he gave into his demons.

Both Suzette and the resources helped me to understand how there could be such a disconnect between Col's two behaviors. Many of those who had been emotionally deprived as children, grew up to not have the correct emotional responses to relationships. These people learned quickly that society did not reward this behavior. They also learned by observing what the correct responses were even though they did not internalize these feelings. They created a persona that would earn them the responses that gave them validation, approval or other rewards. But a large part of the abuser's need is for a scapegoat. It is needed to punish some of the demons.

There was a great need to have someone (or several someones) to blame and since the person usually does not understand who had caused the problems or who had caused the lack in themselves. They have so much misplaced anger that they don't know what to do with, it often goes toward a close family member who is usually a spouse or a child.

I know this is an over simplification of what I learned or we would be on my story for the next few days! So let me get back to my story.

The next two years passed and things seemed pretty much the same.

One day Paula called me up and asked me to come to see her. Well, that was different. She had never done that before. I asked her why and she said she would tell me when I got there. I said the kids and I would be there and she told me not to bring the kids. Now I was really befuddled. Not afraid, just confused.

So, on a Saturday morning, I asked my neighbor to watch Mia and Biff and I drove to Clinton.

Paula said, 'Sit down, I have a lot to tell you.' I sat.

Paula asked me, 'Do you remember my friend Janet? She and her husband Gerry were here one time when you came to visit.'

I shook my head, no.

Paula went on, 'Well, I guess I should not continue to call her my friend. Turns out she has something in common with your husband and mine.'

I sat and just looked at Paula. Trying to comprehend what she was trying to say to me. What would her friend have to do with me or with Col?

Paula said, kindly, 'Lex, both Col and Andy have been seeing Janet. I told Col that if he did not tell you, I would.'

'That's not true', I protested, he doesn't even know her. He hates to come to New Jersey. He never comes over here.'

'Col has been meeting her in Lodi. I found out about Andy because I found a receipt in his pocket. Can you think of anything more stupid? So I did the usual and confronted him. Stupid jerk, Andy admitted it and told me that, of course, it was over, now Janet was seeing Col.

Andy, the clueless clod, thought that telling me about Col would make it all better. This was a month ago. I talked to Col three times and told him to end it and then tell you. I also talked to the Lovely Janet and told her that I would kick her ass to Pennsylvania and back if she called or in any other way communicated with either of them again. I am so sorry to have to be the one to have to tell you. Col is a bigger jerk, if that is possible, than Andy.'

My body just went numb. I couldn't fathom what she was saying. Fidelity was the one thing I thought I had going for my marriage. No other women. Well, now that is gone too. It was complete. I guess Col had had the wine, and the women and I just got a hate song.

Suddenly the most amazing thing happened. This huge weight lifted off me. I had the most incredible, intense feeling of freedom. I had just heard what should be the worst news possible short of a death and all I felt was relief.

The last lynch pin that was holding my marriage together was gone. The last betrayal. I had loved this man so intensely. And over the years he had ground all of that love into the ground. What had been left was a sense of connection based on that last bit, the last shred of what I was holding on to.

I thought that his faithfulness meant something. The last stable belief that I had in a fragile house of cards and it all toppled down in a second.

Paula looked shocked, and said, 'Glory, why are you smiling?' I had not realized that I was. I tried to explain. She looked puzzled and then I just began telling her about the last years. All of the abuse, and all of the neglect and negativity. The dam broke. Everything that I had been keeping inside was spilling out of my mouth. I told her all of it. Slowly, I saw that she understood.

We were both the walking wounded and we would both do what we had to do. She had a marriage to save. I didn't.

Paula asked me if I was OK to drive back to Nyack. I said I was and drove home. A million thoughts crashing and banging around but the one clear thought kept emerging. Free! I was free!

I waited a few days to tell Col what I knew. He already knew that Paula had told me because he had called Janet to set up a meeting and Janet had told him about her conversation with Paula. She was really afraid of Paula and told Col that she would not see him anymore. I guess she moved on to the next married sap.

Col surprised me and was very upset and contrite. More of his old, 'I am sorry, it will never happen again, just give me a chance to prove it to you, please don't leave me now.'

The one thing I agreed with was that I was in no shape to make any life changing decisions. So I agreed to give it one year.

That year started off great in some ways. A new and improved Col. He did not go out. He did not drink to excess. He spent time with the family and we even went a few places and he seemed to interact with the kids. We even took a short vacation to Chicago with the kids.

He would ask me about my classes and asked me to tell him about some of the authors. Then he suggested that we go into the City and go see some of the plays. I had begged for that for years. We took the kids and had a wonderful time. To this day, these outings are some of my cherished experiences as a family. It was a very as close as we ever came to being a happy family. Six months. I liked this new Col. I was fighting to get back to love.

Col gave me gifts. This was very unusual for him. Over the years there had only been a handful of gifts and I could name every one, the occasion and the date. Now he was giving me cards, and on Christmas he stunned me by giving me a mink coat and matching hat. I was truly touched.

What a conundrum this was becoming. Col was offering everything I wanted. I wanted to have that loving place back in my heart. But just like Humpty Dumpty found out, it is impossible to put it back together once it is truly shattered.

I really wanted to make it work. But down deep I knew it could never be the same as it had been in the beginning. No matter how hard I tried I realized that I had changed. Worse was the realization that the Col I really wanted did not exist. He never had.

We had both married blindly, marrying somebody we imagined. Love erodes when it is not nurtured. The sensual part of the love had been pounded out of me both physically and emotionally. One morning I was fixing breakfast and he was sitting at the table complaining about the bacon not being crisp enough and suddenly I was slammed with one of those self realizations that seem to come out of nowhere but are really years in the making. Any feelings I had were gone. Dead in the water. This marriage was not retrievable. Col was Col and I was who ever I had become in the process. I realized that what I really wanted right now was peace. And this would never happen with this marriage.

Too little. Too late. The really sad part was that I was that I could no longer be in love with Col. Maybe some people can go back and rekindle feelings but it's not my bag. I tried, I really did. He was the father of my children and I wanted so much to keep this family together. But every day made me more aware that I did not want to be with him. He had beaten and berated all of the love right out of me.

I had stayed all these years, hoping every day that something would change. Who knew, the change would be in me? I wanted my version of a happy marriage. Didn't happen. Couldn't happen.

I have often wondered what Col's idea of a happy marriage was? I wonder if he had any idea of what that was. Or did he just drift along, hoping I would just keep being Little Miss Stepford Wife, and go along to get along? I don't know.

I was still seeing Suzette. I think it was what kept me from going off the deep end. She helped me get *myself* back. I began to be able to see many things that I had not seen before. She never actually told me to stay or to leave. She told me that I had to look at the future and decide what I wanted. What did I want my life to be like in five years, ten years? That rocked me back on my heels. Suddenly I knew that this life I had now was not what I wanted. And clearly it was not getting better.

The pure irony of this is that while he was ignoring me over the last few years, staying together was possible. Now that he wanted to be physical and communicate, I could not deal with it.

Because of my volunteering at the shelters, I have been to meetings with other abused women and heard this story so many times. Some people are able to go back. Some are not.

The more I resisted, the more intense he became. Suddenly the woman he had abused, demeaned, ignored and had beaten was desirable and wanted. Talk about being on a roller coaster. I think my emotions were as confused as his.

Col convinced me that *I owed it* to him and to the kids to try to fix our problems. So there I was right back in the situation. Boy, can we women fool ourselves. I tried to think of what I could do to try to get back into a loving place.

So, again I went into my salvage mode, choosing to hope when any rational person knew it was useless. What is the definition of insanity?

Doing the same thing over and over, hoping to get a different result. I was seeking a new result with the same old set of behaviors. Self delusional. I wanted things to change. Most of all I wanted to get the old feelings back from the beginning of our marriage.

One day, I said to Col, 'Let's take a trip as soon as my semester is over. You can take the time off. Your partner owes you so many days. Let him run the business for a month. We'll take the kids and do a big turn around the country. Go from here to California. Do it all. Grand Canyon, Disney Land and everything in between.'

Col looked as if I had asked him to wrestle an alligator. 'Stop being ridiculous, Glory, I can't just up and leave and go on a stupid vacation. And we have no business spending that kind of money. The last damn thing I would want to do is be stuck in a car playing tourist. Where do you come up with this crap?'

So the new good times were over. Things were right back where they had always been. Col was his old, angry, morose, sullen self. I could do nothing right. He started getting on the kids, especially Biff.

Sadly, I don't think it would have made a difference if he had wanted to go on the trip. He could have become the most gentle, loving, talkative person. The damage to our marriage had already gone past the point of no return. Any positive fix was long past. We always want to ascribe blame. So whose fault was it?

Maybe I need to take as much blame as I am giving out. I chose a man who could never be what I wanted or needed. We both had baggage that precluded any possibility of a nurturing relationship. And I stayed too long. Way too long.

Everybody around me had tried to tell me, but Oh, NO! I was going to be there for the long haul. And I almost lost whatever "me" I had been discovering and was submerging my personality all over again. I was this pathetic *Stepford Wife*. Clean, cook, take care of everybody else's needs and most important, shut up.

Two weeks later, he came home on a Friday, walked into the bedroom and was packing a bag. As I walked into the bedroom he told me I needed to drive him over to Jack's.

I said, 'May I ask why? knowing that I might be incurring his wrath but felt compelled to ask.

He snarled his answer, 'The guys and I are going to Vegas.'

'How long?'

'When I am back, I'm back. I call you to pick me up. Now, shut up and go get in the car.'

Click!

It was over. What had been dead for a long time could now get a decent burial.

Without a word, I turned, went out sat in the passenger seat, did not say a word, nor did he, we got to Jack's, he jumped out, grabbed his suitcase from the back seat, did not say goodbye, and walked over to Jack's Jeep and was putting his suitcase in as I backed out.

There had been the *click*. It was over, I could no longer deceive myself that I was doing it for the kids or for any other reason. Over was over. I have known women who stayed. You have too. No longer people with any "self" left.

I was going to reclaim the self I had lost over the years. I wanted "me" back. Brash, energetic, ambitious, happy, funny and most of all, without that horrible sense of dread. That feeling in the pit of my stomach that was afraid all the time. I was so tired of worrying about I might do or say that would cause the next violent episode or receive the words that wounded more deeply than the physical abuse?

I am so sorry, BFFs, I have really put a pall on this party. That was not my intent!

Lex, came over and shoved onto the chaise next to me. "Hey, Honey Bun, this is what this evening is all about. You can't let it all go until you let it all out. That's what you told me."

She gave me a bear hug, and told me "Continue, My-Dear-One." I hugged back, and went on, "I drove home, told the kids that we were moving."

They panicked, of course, I told them that they would not be changing schools or friends. I told them that I knew that they would miss their father, I knew that he loved them and that would never change.

He had made an effort for a few months. Now I wanted him to extend those good feeling toward the kids. I just hoped that he would continue to be with them after we worked everything out.

All I knew was that if I did not leave now I would be lost. My sanity depended on it.

I know that is melodramatic but all of you have known women who did not get out when they should have. They are soulless shadows. Walking dead. I don't think that benefits anybody. Especially the children. Oh, I already said that, but it was not an easy decision. This was years in the making. Seems like it was spontaneous. *The click*. No, it takes years to erode those feelings. The click is just when our brain finally let's us know what we really knew all along but just did not want to see it.

You know what? I have thought about taking a sabbatical and doing more research on the topic. Write a book. I have never seen any really definitive study on the issues involved. I know, I would need to work with somebody else with a psych background, but I just wish somebody would do it.

We deal with kids everyday that are products of marriages that are toxic and the children that are poisoned by it.

That day, standing in that bedroom, in a split second, I saw the future. And the sad creature I would become. I just could no longer be afraid all the time. And this was not the marriage I wanted my children to see. Children are not better off in a ruined marriage.

Then I called Mr. Holdenfield at the college because he always knows people who know people. He did. He gave me the number of a rental agent who could find a quick apartment. We were at the Red Roof for nine days and then into the Mt. Holly apartments.

It was a tiny, one bedroom apartment. But it was trauma free. It was mine. I had not even realized how scared I had been all the time until I was living in this abuse free zone for a few weeks. One day, I discovered that the horrible pit-in-my-stomach fear was not there. I did not fear the sound of his car coming into the driveway. The slam of the door or the first bark of his disapproval for something I had or had not done.

Here comes the crazy part. Col got back from Vegas. I had left a note and the number for the room at the Red Roof. He didn't even call.

It was almost a month later that I began to see him every where. His car would be across the street when I left for work. Then I would see him in the parking lot when I left my last class for the day. No calls. Just Col, popping up everywhere I went. Col would be coming around the isle in the grocery store that I went to. This was a man who never went into a grocery story. And this one was nowhere near where he lived. Just near where the kids and I lived now. He would pop up at the gas station, the post office, even the parking lot at the college. It was chilling.

But at the same time it was still not as bad as it had been living with him all of those years. I could take this part.

I called him and he would not talk to me. Stranger and Stranger. He wanted me off balance and it succeeded. Six months of being gas-lighted.

Stuff happened. Tires slashed. Sugar in my gas tank. Tar on the steps out of the apartment. Then my car was repossessed. He had managed to forge my name and borrow money at the bank on *My car*! I went out one morning and there was a guy hooking my car up to be towed. I went ballistic. He showed me papers.

I had to get a taxi to school. I went to the bank after work and guess what! There was a loan, months overdue and my only recourse would have been to have Col arrested and charged with fraud. Well, who does that to their kids father? He won that round.

But here is one that happened before the car was taken. Easter Sunday, I told the kids, let's go to St. Pat's. I was afraid to go to our regular church because Col who never went to church, was showing up every Sunday to the neighborhood church.

We got all gussied up in our Easter duds and drove into the City. Kids were excited and having fun. I had told them that we would go out for a fun lunch and that I had a surprise for them. I had the Easter Baskets in the closet ready to appear as soon as we got home.

We were almost to the G.W. Bridge and a guy in a large Buick must have realized that he needed to cross three lanes of Sunday traffic to get into the correct lane to get to the bridge. This bemoth of a car ran right across the bow of my Chevy wagon. It tore off my bumper and moved me almost into the next lane.

I got the car stopped and onto the shoulder, both Mia and Biff had been knocked onto the floor of the back seat. Remember, this was long before the seatbelt rule. Anyway I got pulled off to the side, retrieved the kids from where they had landed on the car floor, checked them to see if they were OK. Now the demolition car is parked in front of me.

Just as I was getting out of the car, a police car drove up behind me. He walked over with the usual exaggerated, cop-swagger and asked if everybody was OK. I nodded yes. He told me to get out my Insurance Card and Registration.

So I crawl back in the car, go into the glove compartment and start rummaging around. No insurance card. No registration. I get out and tell the cop that I have nothing. Then I tell the cop that I am in the process of a separation and things have been happening such as slashed tires and the sugar incident. He gets the idea very quickly. He says, 'Get back into your car and just sit for a minute.'

I did.

He goes to talk to the driver of the other car. Demolition car leaves. He comes back to my wounded vehicle, stops and pulls the bumper the rest of the way off, tells me to open the back of the station wagon, then told me to drive back home, park the car, and on Monday get somebody to take me to get new registration and insurance.

I had to go through hoops to get that all straightened out and then just a few weeks later the damn car gets repossessed. The car had not even been fixed yet.

Just to add a little more salt in the wound, I had to pay the difference on what the bank sold the car for and what was owed on it. I was barely paying the bills and this was a huge debt.

I guess that was Col's plan. I would have to come crawling back home when I could not make it on my own. Well, I was just as determined that I was not going back. I would do whatever it took to be independent and free from fear, free from abuse and free from feeling worthless. Right then I would have dug ditches as a second job before I would have put myself back into that hot mess.

That was my first year of what I like to refer to as my liberation. It was a mixture Heaven and Hell. Every day I felt more like my own person. The old self was emerging out of that black, tar pit of fear. I could be the same at home as I was at school. I even saw a difference in the kids. I doubt if they were aware of it but they emerged and they talked more and they were much more playful and relaxed at home. They even began to talk and make comments about what was on television. Something they would have never done before.

I did have to worry about his sudden appearances, but at the same time it was still better than the daily oppression. I was beginning to lose that hard knot of fear deep in my middle. Hard to explain.

Col's sudden appearances stopped just as suddenly. One day I realized that I had not seen him anywhere, and nothing bad or nervous making had happened. Not one incident for a couple of weeks. I was waiting for the other shoe to drop. It took me almost two months before I believed that maybe there was a possibility of this being a permanent situation. I began to believe that Col was beginning to accept the situation.

I was even hopeful that he would now be willing to develop a relationship with the kids in our new found circumstances. I called him several times and tried to get him to visit the kids. Col made it very clear that that just was not going to happen.

A new form of punishment. I wanted him to take the kids for visits, so of course he would not. I just could not get him to step up and be responsible. What others needed was just not going to work in his playbook. Once when I begged him to come get the kids and take them out for the day or even overnight his response was, 'I am not going to babysit while you go out and shack up with some scumbag.' So much for father of the year.

Occasionally he would come by, spend an hour with them, and woosh, be gone. Once, Biff asked me why I kept Daddy away. I asked him why he thought I was keeping him away. Biff, pipped up. 'Because Daddy says he can't spend more time with us because you don't want him to.

I wanted to go to his house and he said you made the lawyers fix it so we can't go there anymore.'

I was incensed. But years of experience had taught me that talking to him about it would just make it worse. I tried to talk around it, but got nowhere. There was always an excuse when I suggested any thing to do with the kids.

Sadly now I had another thing to be angry about. And I am sure that I did not handle it very well. Every time I thought I was getting to my *happy place,* Col would do something and snap me right back and then I would be pissed all over again. Sadly, I know it was very obvious to the kids that I was truly angry with him. And he, being Col, suddenly realized that he had a new audience for his good-guy persona. He wasn't around much, but it was enough for the kids to begin to believe that I was the one that made daddy stay away. I was the one that made them do what they needed to do, and Daddy was now Mr. Good Guy, who made these all to infrequent visits a blast. I just couldn't win with him.

I thought I was making a new life that would be better for both me and my children and he was still finding ways to make the kids unhappy. Now they were unhappy that I had taken their father away from them. They thankfully had not been aware of the nightmare I had been living. And being kids they just saw the here and now and who was providing them with fun times and who was the mean parent trying to raise them the best way that I could.

Sadly this part of my story does not have a good ending but I am going to skip over that now. I can talk about the rest of it because I have had years to come to terms with my demons with that marriage. What I don't have right now is the time that I need to fix what is going on with my grown children.

Why doesn't somebody tell us when we are making the choices that these choices will have ramifications. Wouldn't we all just love to have a crystal ball that would let us to see into the future what all of the ramifications will be. But if I am really honest and analytical, I know that from that first choice on I was damned if it did and damned if I didn't.

Somehow over the years, the parent who was there every step of the way and who tried to be the best, but very flawed, parent, has become the bad one and the parent who skipped off into the sunset and returned on his lying white horse and is now Big Daddy. Dammit.

So let me get back to the part that I was trying to tell. I will leave my really sad saga until our next group sharing of *what my kids have done to me*. I don't think that topic has come up yet.

One day after class, I went back to my office and there was a message to call Col at his plumbing office.   He wanted to meet for lunch. I started to decline and he said, 'No this is about the divorce and you *will* want to see me.'

So we arranged to meet Saturday in Paramus, at Altman's Plantation Restaurant. Col said not to bring the kids.

I got Penny to watch them and went to this mysterious meeting. Col looked rested and more like his old self. We sat down and before I could even say anything, he told me that he wanted the divorce to not only go through but to get fast-tracked.

I said, 'That's fine, is there a reason?'

He game me the super-smug Col look and said, 'You're Damn straight, I want to get married. I met a real woman. So let's get this show on the road.'

And that is exactly what happened.

I remember thinking that I were really lucky, someday I would never have to see him ever again! Someday the kids would be grown, they could make what ever connection that they wanted. There was light at the end of the tunnel. Shows how much I knew.

I was just glad that I did not have to be any part of it of his life. Sadly, his life did not include the kids. I was so clueless that I thought it was a good thing and it was so much easier not having to deal with him. Over the years, I tried to get him to visit or let the kids visit. Didn't happen.

I don't know where my head was but I thought they were coping with that very well.

Here comes the shameful part. I was so angry, and there was so much pent up emotion of what had been done to me and now what I perceived to be being done to the kids, that I know way too much of it spewed out of my mouth all too often. I let that anger show. So in that sense, I did become the bad parent. Now, I wish I could shout from the roof tops to tell other newly divorced women to learn to keep quiet. Let the kids grow up and find out on their own. Or not find out. Whatever. Wish I could take that part back. It is my biggest failure. My big regret. Too bad Dr. Spock didn't write a book on that part of child raising.

All I can say Ladies, is that Col is the gift from Hell that just keeps on giving! Somehow I think it will be engraved on my tombstone or urn or whatever I wind up in. Maybe I can just be scattered over the Hudson. My own little gone with the wind.....

I know we all think our own experience is unique. I certainly did. Over the years I have worked with women who are abused, battered, abandoned or in a transitional state that leaves them confused and non-functioning. Yes, the stories are all unique and yet there is a common thread that runs through all of these stories. There are so many self-help books out there but I have yet to see one that really addresses these problems.

Society has only begun to scratch the surface in providing services for women who find themselves in all of the situations. Look at me. I have believed for years that all of this was long behind me and just recently, I have encountered a whole new chapter in this saga. I don't even know what to call it. Long distance abuse? Revisionist marriage and divorce history? I have always had what I thought was a good relationship with the two older kids. Col seems to have decided that he suddenly wants a relationship with them. Now I have two very confused, grown children. It is so fresh and so raw that I am just going to shut up now. This is a topic for a later get-together. Sorry

Sorry, I said that already. See, I am still nuts. But then you knew that didn't you my lovely, supportive, caring, Buddys!

I'm tired. Who is next?"

4:18 AM

There was a long pause. Mora rolled her shoulders, "How about we take fifteen or twenty minutes to stretch. My old bones get stiff so easily now. If I don't walk soon you are going to be carrying me to the powder room."

JJ and Reg pushed the coffee table up snug to the couch and sat on the carpet and began to do an exercise together that looked like an old children's see-saw game.

It occurred to me that the six of us were the embodiment of pure love. Genuine affection among women. Toward each other and within the group. We would tease each other, fight with each other but pity the poor soul who harmed or went against one of us.

Lex came back over and sat on the pillow that was plopped down next to my chaise.

"You know, I do feel better sharing. Just telling my story made me see how much I have been able to let go. I know I have to learn to let the rest of it go. I know I can't change what the kids think. Their memories of events are so skewed that there is no logic I can use to right it. And if I try they think I am just spewing more of the *Hate Daddy Crap*." I let out a long shuddering sigh, "You help me so much by just letting me talk and helping me to see what I need to do to be able to heal. So I hope we are both letting go of some of our baggage. God, I hate being such a boring, whinny witch."

Lex, squeezed my hand. "You did so well with this party, my Love-Bug Buddy. You always nail just what I need. And that cake! Perfect, perfect, perfect!"

"I'm having lunch with Janine tomorrow. She says she has something to tell me. I think she and Patrick are setting a date. I have been so afraid that she and Austin have been afraid of marriage because of the relationship with Hunter. I don't think they remember that much of how it was with Harvey. I think that I have just begun to see that they have been affected by this too. Funny how you don't think of how it affects the kids until it is too late."

"I know", I squeezed her hand back. "But you know all of that, no need to rehash."

"I try to move on. I really do. Then Col does something and I am right back in the soup. Why doesn't somebody tell us that the mistakes we make when we are under Diana's spell will haunt us for the rest of our lives. Nobody gets a pass. Look at all of us."

Lex jumped up, "Hey, Birthday Guests, get your asses back in here and let's revel!"

"We all need some oxygen and loosen up these tired old muscles. Glory just got *Chicago*. I am going to slap the DVD in the old player and we are going to MOVE!"

The group stood up laughing as Lex pulled the disc from the shelf and popped it into the machine and started it. Loud music filled the room. I am really glad that I don't live close enough to anyone who would complain.

Although it would be pretty funny to have somebody call the cops and when the cops, young of course, got here, they would see six, middle-aged college teachers gyrating like thirteen –year-olds.

We were having so much fun, we continued twisting our old bodies into shapes that we would regret the next day. We did our old disco dance moves, laughing as much as what passed for dancing, to three of Chicago's numbers and when Lex turned it off we were renewed and refreshed.

Mora, out of breath and laughing. said, "I am so glad none of my students can see this. I would really have an image problem. By the way Lex, the kids would crack up when you called it a player. I'm surprised you didn't call it a phonograph!"

I answered, "Heck she can call it whatever she wants to! But I was just thinking, what if old Bennett could see us now? He already thinks we are the *Bad Seeds* of the College. At the last faculty meeting, his eyes almost crossed while he was looking down his nose. If it were up to him, all the classes would be taught by visiting Jesuit Priests."

JJ chimed in, "Amen to that sister! Do you know that he actually asked me why I pick literature that is so focused on death and dying. The man has the brain of a tree frog."

There were two answering ribit-ribits and Reg managed a respectable frog belch.

I looked at Lex, "Do you want to suggest the next topic or are you passing?

"I pass. Somebody come up with something fun."

Reg jumped up, "OK, My Ladies of the Evening", oops, I guess I should say night, nay, morning. My, God, where did the time go? We all seem to have gotten a second wind. I love these all-nighters!"

Anyway, I have one that I think is funny. At least it is funny now. You all know that I am a Scarsdale girl.   Born and raised.   I got a scholarship to Fordham right out of Scarsdale Senior High School. Of course, until I went to college and met "real" people, I thought I was very worldly.

I was commuting every day and still pretty well controlled by my parents the same as when I was in high school.

During the summer between my sophomore and junior year, I got a hair up my "bee-hind" and decided that I would go out on my own. I found a room with another student that was actually part of a house in White Plains.

Three bedroom house, two students in each bedroom, everything else shared. Oh yeah.

What a shock. Suddenly Mom was not doing my laundry, not cooking for me, or anything. I was learning that freedom ain't free. Then my dad declared that if I wanted to be "grown" I could damn well pay for my car insurance, rent and some of my own expenses. WOW! Not quite what I had signed up for.

I found a job in a club in Scarsdale. Upscale place but the bottom line was that it was a pick-up joint with a clientele that was better dressed, but the goal was the same old story.

I am the hostess. Whoo hoo! I get to dress up in fancy evening clothes and get paid for it. And for the first few months it really was fun.

I kept hearing the waitresses talking about Mr. Smith and what a jerk he is. Well, the terms that they used for him were a little stronger than that.

One day I am listening to two of the girls talking and I get that this mythical person whom I have never seen, has a "room" upstairs. And it is quite a room. Round bed, purple fake-fur bedspread, mirrored ceiling and an abundance of fancy sex toys. I did not even know that there were sex toys. But I could not bring myself to admit my total ignorance.

I was aware that the workers at the club thought I was an oddity. One of the bartenders called me Babe in Woods, Little Girl Naïve and other cutesy names. But nobody was really mean to me or rude. My father was horrified when he found out where I was working. And I was still young enough then to think that was a good thing. God, we are stupid when we are young.

I had been working there for and about three months when the owner came into the club. I was just seating a couple, when the normal loud din came to an abrupt halt. Eyes were looking past me. I turned and there was a group of men headed toward the bar. The was a clear center of the group.

The man in the center was a burly man, bald, medium height, but he gave off an aura of a much larger, taller man. Grim faced, with eyes that seemed to take in everything, he oozed menace, power, evil.

In my sheltered little life, I had not encountered his kind. Heard about them but I had never even been close. One of the girls came up behind me. 'Close your mouth, Reggie. Go on back to the door. That's Mr. Smith.' *Mr. Smith?* He looked as much like Smith as I looked like Tweety Bird.

I started to scoot back to the front desk and I saw him say something and look directly at me. Scared the pudding out of me.

The man he spoke to came over to the desk and said, 'What's your name, Girlie?'

I stammered out, 'Regina.'

'Come to the office, Mr. Smith wants to meet you.'

'Why?'

'Honey, you don't ask why. You just go to the office. Bring him a Regal straight-up.'

I found the manager, Susan, and asked her if I had to take Mr. Smith a drink to his office and she gave me a very serious look and said, 'You'd better do it.' Then she looked away and found something that required her immediate attention and hurried off.

I was not so naïve that I did not have a clue what was on the agenda. Me! But I was foolish enough to think that I could talk my way out of it.

I went over to the bar side, got the drink on a tray, and went to the office. I knocked and the door was opened by one of the men that had been with him earlier.

Now instead of the shinny, black, Italian Silk suit that he had been wearing, he had on a purple, velvet running suit. Underneath the jacket he was bare-chested. Well, bare except for the heavy, grizzled, chest hair that he seemed to be presenting as a badge of his manliness.

This bit of information Reg presented brought on groans and sighs from the group. JJ made a loud raspberry.

Reg continued, "I squeezed past the gorilla doorman, and set the tray on the desk."

Mr. Smith growled, 'Sit down'.

I chirped, 'Oh, I can't, I am working now.' and I literally ran from the room.

I went back out on the desk, continued my shift and was relieved when it ended and I went home.

My next shift was several days later. As I was changing into the dress I was wearing for the evening, Susan came into our bathroom.   'Girl, that wasn't smart. That man always gets what he wants.   I wouldn't piss him off if I were you.'   I asked her if he were in the club. She shook her head, 'Nope.'

Things went along fine for the next few weeks.

Then one shift, just an hour before closing time, the same thing happened. But this time I was told to take him a drink to the room upstairs.

Whoa! What to do? I was scared shitless. But I wanted to keep the job. Good money, easy, fun place to work, most of the time.

I went, got his drink from Sam and trudged up the back staircase to the infamous room.

Almost the same story.   Gorilla opens door. I enter. Gorilla blocks door. And the lovely Mr. Smith is square in the middle of the famed, purple, fur bedspread with a towel across his middle. Pretty clear nothing is under it except his self delusional claim to manhood.

Lucky for me, he tells Mr. Gorilla to get lost. Tells me to come over and deliver his drink.

My own delusions kick in and I make a little speech to the naked, energized bunny on the bed.

'Mr. Smith,' I intone in my best, good-girl voice, 'I am not that kind of girl. I do not do what I think you have in mind.'

He locks his intense, cold amber orbs into my eyes, with the most menacing stare I have ever seen from a human, answers me. With a shudder, I knew how the gazelle feels in the split second before the first bite by the lion.

'Missy,' he growled and held my eyes, as he stared a hole in me, 'All the girls who work for me do. Always.'

'Well Mr. Smith, this is one girl who works for you who doesn't.'

Without breaking his stare, 'No, I don't think so. Nobody who works for me says no.'

'Well, you have one now,' I finally stammered out. I tried to hold the contact with the cold heat from his eyes, but I couldn't.

'No, I don't.' His cold, guttural voice matched the menace in his eyes. He stood up, dropped the towel, and bare-assed crossed the room to his bathroom.

I'm thinking, 'Wow, good for me, that is all I had to do, just say no.' I fled out of the room and flew down the stairs and suddenly it dawns on me that I was just fired.

Mr. Gorilla, who is standing at the bottom of the stairs, looks surprised to see me, and he goes back up the stairs as I make a mad dash for back to my desk station.

Susan walks over, looking surprised to see me, I tell her what has just transpired. She hissed, "Go tell Sam you have to leave, and to give you twenty out of the till. Then go get in your car and go home. Now! I am going to have Nathan walk you out. Go!'

Now, I was really scared. The full impact of the virtuous little dance I had done with this man suddenly felt like exactly what it was. He was a man who always got what he wanted. I did as I was told, Nathan got me into my car, stood there while I maneuvered out of the parking lot.   I drove like a maniac over the

Tappan Zee bridge, went to a married friends house for the rest of the week and transferred to Fordham. I had a cousin who lived not to far away and I stayed there until I graduated. I came close to transferring to Berkley! I was that scared.

I was afraid for months. I was constantly looking behind me, checking the car when I would go somewhere.

I had angered a shark and I was still in the same waters with it and all of his shark buddies. I was so damn scared, I moved over to Rockland. I was so grateful that I had been working off the books and I had never had to give the club my social security number. It was years before I ever even told my dad what had happened. He said he thought I had moved because of a broken relationship.

So that is how I wound up over here. After I graduated, I just never moved back to Westchester. I definitely never saw those gorillas again.

Yes, JJ, you can stop smirking, I know all of you know who he was. I was probably the only human on earth who did not. I did not know who he was until a couple of years later and I saw his picture in the paper when he was being tried for tax evasion. The old sot got convicted. Then somebody got him in prison.

When I saw the Sopranos for the fist time, I had to stop watching it. Scared the crap out of me all over again.

JJ gave a snorty laugh and said to Reg, "You know girl, you just told a scary, funny story. You may be the only one who ever got away. But think how lucky we are that you moved over to Rockland. Ha! Westchester's loss!

Lex looked pensive. I reached over and gave her a little punch on the arm.

"What are you thinking about?

Lex looked up and said, "I know this is weird, but I had this story kicking around in my head. I sort of tuned out when my Brit Lit class was emoting and I started hatching this story about one of our illustrious leaders. So it has continued to ferment and form in my fertile little brain. Like a bad song you can't get rid of. JJ's story made me think about the idea of power. If you think about most of the stories we have told all night, most of them have had men in power who take advantage of that power toward others. I'll tell my silly story but your are going to really think I am losing it. My mind just goes to strange places sometimes. You can stop me anytime it gets too weird for you."

All of you know that I remember everything I read or hear. I have never known if this is a blessing or a curse. I read a story a long time ago that another teacher wrote. Over the years it has become a new story in my head. So at this point it is collaboration. I no longer even remember what I read and what I have added. Every time I have had to go listen to our sadly inadequate leader over the past six years of his non-leadership, a little more of this story has formed. So I hope that by telling it now, maybe I can stop adding to it and it will just go into my mental file cabinet with the rest of the useless crap I have accumulated. But don't say that I did not warn you!

The Emperor of Sameness

Once upon a time in a land, really not that far away, and actually not even that long ago, there was a small village, a very small village.

And that village had a school of higher learning. Some people thought that the idea of higher learning was questionable and some thought that even the learning was questionable.

The village was called Anywhere and the School was called The School for Higher Learning. Catchy, huh?

Anywhere was a very peaceful community, with behaving plebeian, pleasant people who always loved each other but sometimes they did not like each other very well. The school was run by a group of village elders. They were selected from among the pleasant people.

It was their job to confer and then rule about what the children would (or would not) learn. Unfortunately, they were subject to much error. A prevalent perception among these peaceful plebes was that they always knew best.

Another perception was that teachers were lowly creatures who did not know best, ever, and must be guided and ruled by those who did not know how to teach or even know the subject matter."

Now our little group was roaring with laughter. "You go, Lex! You just nailed old frog-face." shrieked Mora.

Lex laughed herself, and waved her hands to shush us, then continued, "The elders thought it was not important to know the subject matter."

Lex pulled herself up to her full height and shifted into a perfect pose that created our arrogant, inept leader's usual pose. "What was important was that the children should not learn anything dangerous like independent and should I say the word, "different" thought. These precious offspring and future taxpayers or tax payer recipients of tax welfare monies, must turn out to have exactly the same thought as the knowledgeable elders. They knew best."

Right smack dab in the middle of all of this sameness and continuity of no-new-knowledge and peaceful pastoral plebeiality ascended an event that we call highly special. Was this the birth of a winsome, wailing, waif willingly wafting her warbling wails wildly on the wind? NO! It was not!

Into the village of Anywhere came a new leader. He was more plebeian than any other common plebe. Which made him the perfect person to lead the other common folk and take charge of the silly teachers who might otherwise get carried away on the wings of creativity and independent thought.

Ted the Tiresome came in to help the common folk control this heretic possibility. Ted the tiresome, or TT as his friends called him, was actually more plebeian than all others. As a child, he had always been ineligible for jousting due to low marks in the castle courses in a school that actually admired original thought and actions.

He vowed to keep new ideas from happening in any school that he would lead. And with a pretended boldness, and behavioral bravado, he charged into meetings and proclaimed all new ideas as heresy. Ah, he reaped faultless, fearless, feats of fame! How the non-achievers loved him. Pointless programs of no priorities. He was the keeper of sameness."

The group was giggling and rolling on the floor and saying, "You go girl!" "Boy, do you have our fearless leader pegged." I shushed everybody and told Lex to continue.

Since he had been elected to this high office by the important people of Anywhere, he knew that it was his duty to bring mediocrity to everyone. He must even convert the most egregious offenders, the enemy of the people, the teachers. He spoke in his sonorous voice that he would lead them into darkness.

But this timorous leader had one huge obstacle impeding his goal. He did not under-stand when the teachers talked to him about achieving, and knowledge, and thoughts, and real leadership, and succeeding, and worst of all creating. He had no clue what they were talking about.

He declared that think-tanks were to be rooted out and banned. Talking in class was banned. Work-groups were banned.

Rooms were to be set up with desks in tidy rows and was to be ABSOLUTELY no talking. Not even by the teachers. Text books, those chosen for their lack of ideas and thought-provoke-less content would be read silently and work sheets would be completed.

He would heroically stamp out all progress and high performance. After all, how would that make the low performance students feel? Low achievers should not have to fear the high achievers. He could relate to that and it was his job not to let that happen to any more non achieving students.

He was quite proud of the fact that he did not understand any of the issues that these irritating and rabble rousing teachers wanted him to understand. It was his right, nay, it was his duty to stamp out progress and keep the status quo.

It has worked for thousands of years. Well, maybe not, a citizen of Anywhere told him. Actually there had been progress in the world. Well, he responded in his best sonorous voice, it was time to stop this pesky progress.

Lex was having to talk louder to go over the laughing ladies. I shushed them again so that she could go on.

Undaunted, TT has continued his search for the Holy Grail of Mediocrity. He has continued to flail unfailingly at success. He will not fail to fly feverously in the face of foul fate to felicitously file unfazed fealty to his favorite goal; that each year, the school will fail to exceed the last. And with that he will leave his mark.

Oh, were you expecting a happy ending, my fellow miscreants of trying to pursue excellence? If you were, then you haven't been paying attention.

A resounding burst of applause and hugs all around. Reg said, "I know why your students love you. I think I want to take your Brit Lit class!"

Mora said, "Just talking about him and I need a potty break."

JJ said that we should just call it like it was. "He is the King of Crap."

5:36

Everybody got up to stretch, get needed drinks or candy fixes and just move around. Mora dashed to my study to make a phone call.

I looked at Lex and asked if our *presentations* had to be about only ourselves or could we tell other stories.

"Honey, do what makes you happy. You planned this night and so far it is glorious. I am a very happy camper."

I addressed the group. "I have a question for you all. Everybody can vote. OK, we can stop now if everybody is tired. Go get our beauty sleep. We have all knit up our raveled selves"

"I love you all. You have no idea how much you saved me when Vivian died. I could never have gone through that without all of you. You let me fall apart. So much of the time I had to hold it together for her children. I know how much it meant to them too."

I am going to Connecticut to the farm tomorrow, well, today actually, and be with her kids. Mine are coming too.

The cousins have really been there for each other. Talk about a bittersweet time."

Suddenly JJ and Reg got to me then everybody else grabbed on and we did a group hug with a little dance going on too. Soon we were a blob of middle-aged BFFs in a emotional, drippy mass.

Finally Lex pushed us away. "So, what do you old broads want to do?" Mora piped up, "I don't know about anybody else, but I was sleepy an hour ago and then I got a second wind. I am so pumped that I have no desire to go home. I want stories. Give me stories!" The rest of us laughed and agreed with Mora.

"Lex gave me a long, steady look, then said very quietly, "Glory, don't you think it is time to share Viv's story?"

I looked at all of them, tenderness, tears and love shinning in everyone's eyes.

OK, my lovelies, you asked for it. I don't think I have ever talked this much at one time. Not even in class and if you ask my students they think I talk endlessly.

All of you thought that Viv lead a fairytale life until the cancer that she fought and lost. How she fought. You all know.

Loosing my sister, my rock, was truly the worst thing that has ever happened. In my life, in her family's life. She was always there for us. From day one. *My Big Sis*. Of course I could not imagine life without her. I still can't. If it were not for all of you I would not have survived her death. I would not be able to be there for her kids either.

On the way home from school yesterday, I punched in her number before I remembered. Last week I heard something on the news and my first thought was, gotta call Viv about that.

During the last weeks, when it was clear that her battle was nearing its end, she told me that she had written something and she wanted me to read it. She had given me a folder before she went into the hospital. She had alluded to a letter that she had written and needed to give it to me.   I still thought it contained a letter to me about her children.

It turned out to be a letter that she had written about a part of her life that I never knew about. She said that she had written it, and was going to give it to me so many times but she had put it off.

She didn't give it to me until she had to go into the hospital for the last time.

I have it. I have carried it with me ever since I got it. I would like to read it to you just the way she wrote it. I am not betraying her confidence. You will see why at the end.

I, got up, went to my oversized bag that I call my "life-bag" and pulled out a sapphire blue folder.

"Get comfy, Lassies, its another long one." and I began to read Viv's letter to that she had written to me. It was still so raw and so painful that I was not sure I could get through the whole letter without breaking down. But it was time to tell Viv's story.

Dear Glory,

I know that I should have told you all of this before. I wanted to so many times. I made so many excuses. I told myself that I did not want to burden you with the situation and that I did not want to saddle you with any more of my problems. But I think the real reason was that I did not want you to think less of me. I knew what I was doing was wrong on so many levels and I knew you would have the wiser, cooler head. I did not want you to tell me what I should do. What I knew already.

You have already gotten the letters that I wrote to you about you and me, my love letter to you.

You have gotten the letters that I wrote to you about my precious children.

But this letter was written almost two years before those letters. Ironic. I could not even write this letter until a year had passed after the last time I saw Ash. Yes, Glory, there was an Ash and soon it will be clear who he was. I held on to the original letter for so long, that just before I gave it to you, I had to rewrite it.

When I was pretty sure what the outcome was going to be from this horrible thief of a disease, I knew that I should talk to you about what had happened. But I just kept putting it off. I don't know why, but it just never seemed to be the right time. So I will begin again.

I came close to giving the first letter to you so many times. But each time I tried, it did not seem like the exactly right time. I know, I died a coward's death a thousand times.

Remember right after I had been diagnosed with the Big C? You and I had gone to see the specialist in the City.   We were sitting in the waiting room and we were talking about life's choices.   I had the letter in my purse.   Every time I touched that monster bag, it felt as if it were filled with burning hot coals from Hell.   I missed another opportunity to give it to you and more important, I missed another opportunity to talk to you about this event in my life.

I wish I would have talked with you.   I know you would have told me that I did not get cancer as a punishment for this horrible choice that I had made.

For the past year, I have been obsessed with the idea that some world force, call it God, or call it Karma, whatever it is, I feel as if I have had to pay for my sins.

So I will tell you about it as I remember it. From the beginning.   Just where I think it started. Almost five years ago.

I know that you are asking yourself how you could have not known.   Well, this was the one thing in my entire life that nobody ever knew about except for Ash and me.   And the only redeeming part of this story is that I think I did the right thing in the end.   It helps me to know that I did not cause pain for my children or for Damon. They did not deserve to be hurt over what I chose to do.

I guess I *am* starting at the end. I remember sitting at my kitchen counter in front of my laptop. I was trying to concentrate on returning some email messages. I was not having much luck.

All I could think about was the letter that I had written to Ash. He would have received it by now. How had he reacted? Had he expected it? Had it hurt as much to read it as it had hurt me to write it? Maybe he was even relieved. I just wanted to rush to the phone and hear his voice, see how he was. I wanted to be able to fix it if he was in the same pain I was. But I knew with all my being that this was not an option.

I have never known this much emotional pain before. I used to think that when people said they hurt and had a broken heart, that it was just a figure of speech, not a true physical feeling. Now I know.

I have not been able to stop crying. I know I have to hide it. Now I know what the phrase, *crying on the inside*, means. It is there, just bubbling under the surface and the least thing sets me off. I was so glad that Wes and Damon had done their usual mad scramble before they left. Neither of them had looked at me before rushing out to begin their day.

Neither had even noticed that I had not said a word. I had just made the usual breakfast, both had chewed and gulped at warp speed, slugged down juice and coffee, Wes grabbed a school bag, Damon grabbed his briefcase, whoosh, the door slammed, and I was alone. For once I was so grateful for an empty house.

How had my life become so out of control? My actions had changed my comfortable, safe life with its predictable days. One meeting, one chance encounter had plunged me into this pretty pass.

I am not blaming anybody. And if truth be told, I am not even entirely blaming myself. I think my choice was destined. Not by something mystical. Just by the circumstances that have been my life.

I wanted to call you so many times, tell you everything and let you reassure me that everything would get better.

I also knew that I wasn't ready to talk during the time I spent with Ash. As I was ending it, I knew that the only person that I wanted was Ash. But if that if I had heard his voice I would have been lost. Ash would be lost. And we would have hurt so many innocent people.

I know this is all very melodramatic. But that is what life is. Lots of drama and sadly, messy. We all make decisions that lead us in a direction for good or for ill.

I had nobody to blame for my drama except me. I did this to myself. And I really don't know if I could have made a different decision. Either to begin it or to end it.

So I am going to have the luxury of a good wallow in how this came about and then I will try to not only pick up the pieces but try to glue them back together again.

So where did this begin? At the beginning of course! If something is ended it has to have a start, right?

Glory, you have always said that I was the Happy-Ever-After girl. I had the perfect husband, the perfect children, the big house in

Connecticut, hadn't worked since I married, I had it all. I was a walking, talking cliché. I never complained to anyone when things were bad for me because I didn't know how to make anybody understand. Not even you, Glory. You used to tease me and call me the Princess of Perfect.

It always sounded so petty if I complained about my life. I always envied you with your purpose-filled life. You changed lives and had people admire you for what you did and not for what you had or how much money your husband made. I know what problems you had with Col but you were solving your problems. I never doubted for a minute that you would land on your feet. I thought of you as Wonder Woman. You see a problem, you charge in and slay it.

As you know, Damon's company was already successful when we married. I had never been a part of it. He told me, much more often than I wanted to hear, that he just wanted me to enjoy what he had worked for. I tried so many times to tell him that I wanted to do something with my life. And he would look at me and tell me that I did not need to do anything because he took care of everything. And he did.

Damon was never mean or hurtful on purpose. He was neglectful but he never realized that he was. He was doing the manly thing. He was slaying the beast and bringing it home. The big problem was that I did not even have to take care of cooking the beast or cleaning the cave. Somebody else did that too.

Not long after we married, I had Jeffery. My first born joy. Then the other then my other two precious children. Three children in five years. What happy years.

Then one day I woke up and realized that the children had lives of their own and they did not need me nearly as much. My job was almost done. And as the next few years passed quickly and I was less and less needed.

Wesley was the only one at home and he spent his time divided between his buddies and sports with whatever was left for his girlfriend, Donna.

We saw Jeffery and Heather on school breaks.

Heather was working toward her medical degree and marriage was not even close to the top of her agenda.

Jeff was engaged and Marilyn's mother was having blast planning the wedding. I was told that my job was to just show up in my mother of the groom regalia and enjoy myself.

My house ran itself. Maids cleaned, Cook cooked, and I had run out of rooms to decorate and ideas to re-decorate. I did not play cards, drink or have obsessive hobbies.

I had gone so far as to suggest to Damon that we could think about having another child. We could adopt.

He laughed, not unkindly, and told me to take up photography or get a realtor's license or something. I don't think that he meant to be cruel. I just think that men do not understand the problem. We are a non-communicating species. I tried so many times to talk to him about my feelings of not being needed. And he would say, 'I need you', and then every action of his would demonstrate that I was not needed.

So I began to fill my days with museums, art galleries, committees and charity projects.

One achingly, beautiful, fall day, I decided to go into the City and go to an exhibit at the Guggenheim. I spent a glorious hour there and then walked over to the Metropolitan to go to my regular haunt, the Impressionists. After a while I had wandered to look at another favorite. I was sitting on the bench in front of Johannes Vermeer's *Young Woman with a Water Pitcher*. Somebody sat down next to me. I really did not pay much attention. We sat in silent "stranger companionship" both of us seeming to be engrossed in the visceral beauty of this piece.

'Mesmerizing isn't it?' I twisted around to see the face that belongs to the deep, vibrant voice. I was looking at a young Tom Sellick. Sounds silly now but at the time that was the thought that flashed though and yes, he was drop-dead handsome.

I know, I should have run like Hell. Easy to see that now. How much clearer could it have been? A bored, neglected housewife, a gorgeous, attentive man.

Formulaic. But the tragedy is that nobody ever sees the big picture. I just saw an damned attractive man who seemed to have the same appreciation for art that I did.

I could not drag Damon to anything to do with any of the so called arts unless he saw a possibility for new business.

I was intrigued with this man. Obviously cultured, liked the arts, and his manner was not aggressive, just friendly. We were two strangers sharing a moment. He was dressed exquisitely, so I assumed employed, yet, he was here on a bench on a week day. I wanted to know more about this man. Without any conscious thought or decision, we had made that first move toward our involvement.

Well, I can gloss over the next few weeks. Ash, for Ashford, was a brain surgeon. He was always off on Wednesday afternoons and instead of golf he was a museum hound. He said it was his peaceful respite in a very busy, demanding life.

His home story? He had two almost grown sons, both in med school. His wife had Lou Gehrig's disease and he had been trying to juggle his work load while trying to spend time with her.

His Wednesday afternoons at the museum were his only oasis of calm in a life that was consuming him.

It all began so innocently. For months, we met every Wednesday at one of the museums. Had lunch, then spent hours talking endlessly about everything. Our lives. The Arts. The world. Our kids. It was the first time in years that a man had been interested in anything I had to say. My opinions. That is heady stuff.

So, my dear sister, you have figured out by now that this was written for you. I know you will share it with your cohorts. I want you to. And it goes without saying that I never want Damon or the children to ever know any of it. And I know they won't.

You and I are so connected. I know that for all of my life, you are the one person that has always been there. You have always had my back.

This letter is not to justify anything. I know that you will understand. You always understood me better than I did myself.

I hope that I am not burdening you with this story. I don't think I am. I just want you to know something that I should have told you. I feel like I owe you this truth about me. Here it is, warts and all. You have always thought I was perfect. My Sweet Sister, I am not perfect, I am flawed. My perfect marriage was not perfect.

Glory, I know that you won't judge me *too* harshly. As I said, you have always understood me. Somehow I even think you understand me enough to know why I did what I did. We have both made some choices that we have regretted. I think we have always been looking for that total acceptance and love. Ironic isn't it that the one perfect love in both of our lives has been with each other? You and I have been a perfect team. Always there, always doing exactly what the other needed. How did I ever get so lucky that I had you in my corner? You have always been my *forever* person. Remember that even in eternity, I will be there watching over you. Now it is my turn to be the *guiding light* in your life.

Back to *the affair*, funny I never thought of it that way while it was happening. Just after it was over.

I would like to think that there was something exquisitely unique and justifying about this relationship. The reality is that we were two, lonely, wounded people who found each other when we were at our lowest ebb.

One Wednesday, I told Ash that I would not have to rush out because Damon was in Boston for the rest of the week. He got very quiet for a few minutes. Then he asked if I liked the Village. I said of course, but I had not been there in years.

'Then lets get out of here and go enjoy ourselves. I know a great little place there for dinner. I just need to make one phone call.' He walked a little away but I could hear him asking Betty's caretaker if she could stay for the evening. I guess, she said yes, because he walked back smiling, grabbed my hand, and we rushed down the Met steps. We cabbed to the village and spent a glorious time walking in the fading light.

Dinner was fun and funky at a little hole in the wall place with incredible giant meatball sandwiches and egg creams. Soft candlelight gently washed over the sidewalk table. Food smells competed with the usual summer aroma of the village. We laughed about everything. We laughed about the way we were both dressed. We looked uptown while everyone around wore attire that screamed Village.

In an few hours, we had talked more than I had talked with Damon in months.

Ash paid the bill, and said, 'Let's walk.'

We walked up Mott street and joked and laughed at all of the sights and window displays. Ash looked at me, pulled me into a little shop, and said, 'Pick something so we look "Village.' He told the clerk that he would be back and just get the bill ready. I tried on a pair of jeans and a gauzy top. Perfect. Found a pair of flats. Added a belt and I pronounced myself much less Connecticut. Just then he bounced back in clad in Wranglers, village boots and a black turtleneck shirt. We could not stop laughing. The clerk looked amused and had a smirky smile while she rang up my choices. She handed me a wildly colorful bag that held my "lady" clothes. Ash stuffed my bag into his and we sailed out of the little, funky shop.

By the time we walked through the Washington Square Arch it had been dark for hours. Neither of us even mentioned going home. We had never been together outside, or during evening hours. But it seemed natural and that we had been doing it for all of our lives.

There was an unasked question that hung in the air. Suddenly it was midnight. We cabbed back uptown and arrived at the Waldorf.

I don't need to tell you that I had a glorious year. Oddly, I was not guilt-ridden or conflicted in anyway. The mind has a marvelous way of justifying human behavior.

Ash found a sublet in the 90s not too far from the museums. A beautiful brownstone with a tiny back yard. He worked some kind of magic and managed to free up his Sundays.

Damon did not care that I was gone because he just had one less day that he had to feel guilty about. He worked every weekend with very few exceptions. It seemed like the more successful he became, the more obsessed he became with the business.

Wes was immersed in his activities and he seemed to be home only to sleep. He rarely even ate at home and seemed irritated if he was asked to sit down for a meal. So of course, that was one more justification of my own actions.

I know, Sister Dear, I can hear what you are thinking. Oh, I wanted to share with you so many times. But I guess I knew that you would tell me how stupid I was being and how much I was risking. So I never did. See, we know each other so well. I didn't think I was being stupid, except when that little voice in my ear (yours) would whisper, 'Maybe this is not a good idea,' but I would shake it off.

I was able to compartmentalize. And rationalize. For a while we were both as happy as possible under the circumstances. Blissfully, ignorantly. We thought we were not hurting anybody.

Then Betty started getting worse. Much worse. Ash finally had to accept the fact that she had to be hospitalized for the final stages of her illness. We cut back to just Wednesdays because Ash spent Sundays in the hospital with Betty. On Wednesdays, we just met for lunch.

Then one day Ash said that he would have to forgo the Wednesdays. I understood.

The call came, sooner than I had expected that Betty had died. I knew that it would be a while before we saw each other again. We would make do with phone calls. Now Ash called every morning. It was enough just hearing his voice. This went on for eight months.

Then one day, Ash said, we have to meet at the brownstone. I was surprised that he had kept it all this time.

I spend hours choosing what to wear, dressing and anticipating.

This began a new period of our relationship. After about a year Ash wanted me to come to the City more often. I told him that I couldn't do that. It wasn't that I didn't have the time. Time was all I did have. But I knew that I was already too invested in this relationship.

I don't know what would have happened to our relationship if Ash had not changed the situation.

One evening, he suggested going back to the little café in the Village. While we were lingering over our egg creams he suddenly looked very serious.

Ash took out the familiar blue tiffany box. He handed it to me. I knew I did not even need to open it to know what was inside. But I did open it.

The most beautiful blue diamond solitaire knocked my breath out.

Ash said that he knew I could not take it now. We had a lot that would have to happen. He just seemed to take it for granted that the next step would be that I would leave Damon, leave my life, change everything.

I went home and spent a sleepless night. There really wasn't anything to decide except how I would end what I had with Ash. I knew it would break my heart and I was fairly sure that it would be the same for Ash.

I also knew that to do anything else, would wreck more lives. Damon had not done anything wrong, just be a hardworking, goal-driven, pursuer of the American Dream. None of the children would have been able to handle this now either. How could I have ever explained to them why I was unhappy enough to divorce their father.

Jeff was married and expecting. Heather had finally found her true love and they were very close to an engagement. Wes was going off to college.

This ring was a wake-up call. It meant that a choice had to be made. I knew that I could never see him again.

This pain is my punishment. I think Ash is in pain too. But it will be mine and Ash's pain, only. Damon will never know. I am glad Betty never knew. None of the children have to know that I was so unhappy that I was drowning. Now I am drowning in loss and what I have done to Ash. I should have seen what was coming. Nothing ever comes without a price. How stupid of me to believe that what we had would not have a consequence.

My way of telling you, my wonderful, incredible sister is to give you this. I still can't talk about it. At least not yet. Give me time and then we will talk about it. I hope there will be time to talk about it.

Right now I have another battle to fight. I thank my lucky stars every day that I have my children, Damon and you. I could not get through this without you.

I am going to give this to you tomorrow. I am going to ask you to put it away until I ask you to read it and you and I can talk about it then.

You might have to read this if I am gone before I can discuss it with you.

I hope you will understand and forgive me if I have disappointed you with this story. Somehow, I know that you will understand. We were always close because we only had each other. I even followed you to the east because we had that unbreakable bond. I think you chose the better path. You have made your life so much more meaningful.

Do you have any idea how much I love you? You and my children are my purest relationships. Unconditional love.

There is a ring in the envelope. It is the ring that Grandmother Johanna gave me when I married Damon for the *something old*. Please wear it. That unbroken circle. Nothing can ever take that away from us.

I love you Glory. And someday we will sit on a fluffy white cloud and talk and talk and talk.

Your sister, ever after,

Viv

Everyone was crying by the time I finished Viv's letter.

Sadly, we never talked about it. Life got in the way. And then death.

She found out about the cancer and that consumed everything. I know she started to tell me many times. I knew for years that there was something. Ironically I started to talk to her about it many times. But I wanted her to tell me what it was in her own time. There had been a genuine shift in her happiness. So that made me happy. We never discussed it, but I had thought for years that she had been neglected in her marriage. Oh, I knew that Damian was a good guy, but driven in his own way, and that resulted in Viv becoming less needed. I had even tried to bring up the topic of getting her interested in teaching. By then she had seemed to be coming out of the funk she had been in.

Time passed and so many missed opportunities for us to talk about what we should have. Then she found out that she was ill. I think she knew from the very beginning what the outcome would be. She put on a happy, hopeful front, but I think she did not believe she would beat it.

I did not want to push her while she was ill. And the illness went so fast. She was diagnosed in February and she was gone before Christmas. We didn't even have that last holiday with her.

I don't even know Ash's last name. I wish she would have told me in the letter. I would have called him. I imagine he knows, Viv's death was in all the papers. She is buried in the New Canaan Cemetery.

My guess is that Ash may have even come to the cemetery. I wish I could have met him. I can't imagine what he has had to go through. He lost a wife and then he lost Viv. I know that they had to love each other. A Beatrice and Benedict love with a Romeo and Juliet ending.

I am glad that she had the happiness that they had and I am so sorry that she had the grief and then the horrific, nasty cancer that kept her from having happy years left. Life, death. Mankind's story. What we teach everyday. This was just the real deal.

You want to know what is really ironic? Cruel? Damon has quit working the insane hours that he did. He now spends so much time with

Wes. Both of then need each other now. He spends as much time as he can with the other two as well. Just what Viv wanted all those years.

I looked up. Tears were streaming down from all eyes. My throat was constricted by trying to hold back a bout of crying that if it started would consume me.

Again Lex came over and crawled into the chaise with me and wrapped her arms around me. No words. We all stayed quiet for what seemed like a long time. Lex took a tissue out of her pocket, dabbed my eyes then hers. We shared a shaky laugh and then I wiggled to the end of the chase.

Now there was a pile-on with all six of us on my poor chaise. It had never seen such action.

JJ lifted my hand and looked closely at the ring. She didn't say anything. Just patted my hand.

I wiggled out of the pile and jumped up. "I would like to throw out an idea for this little section for our segments as Reg called them.

Let's do more "The story in a letter". Long, short what ever floats your boat. Mora, you want to give it a shot?"

"Funny you should bring that up," Mora said as she stood up and stretched. Looks of loving indulgence passed within the group, "I wrote one for Melody's last birthday. I think I can rise to your challenge, Oh-Wise-One." as she smiled at me tenderly.

Letter to my first born.

Melody Shannon McDougal

Monday's Child is Fair of Face

The Day You Were Born,

March 17, 1975

Friday

Your birth story begins on March 14th. I woke up early in the morning, on Friday, and I was having back and stomach pains. Not really bad but definitely "pains". I had been told that sometimes when you begin labor it feels like gas pains and this did not feel like that. So I just chalked it up to the fact that because I was getting close to giving birth, everything was heavy and pressing down.

I was so anxious for you to be born. This was back in the dark ages and nobody knew what they were having until the doctor said, "It's a girl!" or "It's a boy!" I wanted a girl. I did not even have a reason why, I just wanted my baby to be a girl. I was not afraid of giving birth. Not because I was brave. It was because I did not know anything.

Back in the dark ages, there was no resource to tell you what was going to happen. No books on childbirth. There was a book on taking care of babies and I had been reading it for months. It was the Doctor Spock Baby Book. No, not the one from Star Trek. The baby doctor.

But the "pains" continued and even began to get a little more intense. I finally went next door to my BFF of the time, Nadine, and told her what was going on. She said she thought I might be in labor. But Nadine had never had a baby so she did not know any more than I did. We were the blind leading the blind. So we sat and talked the afternoon away.

Your father came home from work around five and I told him what had been going on. I made dinner and then we finally decided that it might be a good idea to go to the hospital.

Since your father was in the Air Force in the third year of his four years in service you were to be born at the military hospital. The word hospital is a little too fancy for what the building was at McGuire AFB at the time. It was a large rectangular building that housed the OBGYN clinic on one side and the delivery part on the other side.

214

Back in those days, the birthing mother was taken in to the room where you would be in labor until the time to go into the delivery room. Cleverly, it was called a labor room. I do not know where the fathers went.

By now it was late in the evening. And it was a small room with one bed. Nothing else in the room. Not even a bedside table with water or anything. I could hear much yelling and screaming all from the other little rooms. I did not know how many other women were in labor but by the sound it was a lot. And now I was scared. My pains were not that bad but I had a clue that this was going to be a bumpy ride.

Every so often a nurse would come in and check on me. And they would ask how I was doing. How was I doing? How did I know? I had no clue how I should be doing or what to expect.

I tried to get somebody, anybody to explain to me what was happening and what would be happening. But mostly, the nurse would just pat me on whatever part of me was nearest to where they were standing and say, "Well, Dear, you will have to discuss that with the doctor." Only one problem. No doctor came in to my little solitary confinement.

Because this was the military, I had seen several doctors. But mostly Dr. Irving. A little, short, balloon shaped man. Perfectly round. He had a little half halo of hair at the base of his skull that wrapped around to his ears. Everything else was bald and shiny. He was about an inch or so shorter than I was. But I liked him. He was always kind and did not seem as brusque as some of the other OBGYN doctors.

But it was the 70s and I had never asked the questions that I should have asked. Women were not encouraged to participate in their own health care and that included birthing. I did not have a clue about what was going to happen except for my observations when I was in the hospital when I was a teenager and my sister had a baby. All of these had gone quite well, and what I knew was toward the end of the process and the mothers had usually been sedated by local drugs or what was called a saddle block.

Of course I had seen horses and cows giving birth. And that had always seemed relatively easy. And a few times when a vet had to be called my dad had removed me from that so I did not know what went on if there were complications. Somehow I had it in my head that it would be rather easy and if not they gave you something and then you had a baby.

So much for easy.

I asked the nurses for something to read. They said no, nothing can come in the room because it would not be sterile. OK. Finally I went to sleep. Slept fine. So the pains could not have been that bad.

Saturday

I Woke up the next morning and I was totally surprised that there was no baby. Everybody I knew who had gone to the hospital had had a baby within a matter of hours. Nobody had had over a day of labor.

I was still trying to get answers but the nurses kept saying, you're OK, it will happen soon. They kept checking to see if I was dilating any more. I wasn't. And I did not like the checking part. But, I was prepped and so ready to go. But I wasn't going anywhere. Not to the delivery room anyway.

The entire day passed. Nothing. I began singing to my self every time there was a contraction. There were contractions, about every fifteen minutes or so. I ran through every show tune and song I knew. I started making up songs and then I began my playlist all over again. The day passed. The night passed. Still no baby. Still no further dilating.

Sunday

Dr. Irving finally came in sometime Sunday. By now I had lost track of time. No windows, no clock. I was completely isolated except for the hourly check by the nurses. Every time a nurse would come in I was asking what time it was. And occasionally they accompanied me to a bathroom. Down a hallway. A long hallway. But it was like being out of jail and I was enjoying both the walk and the mini freedom. One nurse in particular was very nice and very sympathetic. She asked me how old I was and seemed surprised when I said eighteen. Did she think I was younger? Older? She walked out before I could ask her.

Dr. Irving checked me and he said that I had not dilated any further since the day before. And he was going to call in one of the other doctors.

I don't know the other doctor's name, only that he was the head of the OB at the hospital.

He checked me and said, "She is not dilating because she can't. She needs Pitocin." By that time it was late in the evening, They came in and got every thing started. It was a fluid drip.

And that is when it began. Now it was real, real labor. But for some reason nobody seemed to be monitoring me. But I also was determined that I was not going to be one of the screaming, moaning women I had been hearing all this time. So I rode it out with as little sound as I could make.

After what seemed like an eternity but was really days of mostly boredom and frustration, all Hell broke loose.

Monday, March 17, 1975

I found out later that everything happened around 5 AM.

A huge, giant gut wrenching pain hit, and I guess instinct kicked in because I reached down to the source of that pain and I felt a head. I knew that was the baby. I let out a blood curdling scream, and yelled "Come help me!"

I hear the muted footsteps of the rubber-soled nurse padding toward the room and the door opens, the light floods on and then she screams, "Get the doctor, get a cart! The baby's crowning!" I did not know what that meant but I hoped that the Calvary was coming.

Dr. Irving comes flying into the room as fast as his little, short, legs would carry him. He reaches the bed just in time to do what baby doctors are supposed to do. He was a baby catcher. I was up on my elbows and the push came from somewhere, nobody had said push, but something deep within my body responded to that primal urge to get that baby out.

Push I did, and suddenly you were in the doctor's hands. Another nurse comes into the room pushing a cart that has a tray of instruments. Doc yells, dump the tray!. Nothing happens. He reaches back with and elbows it up, instruments clattering all over the tile floor and the tray is now clear of all instruments.

Dr. Weiner places you on the tray so that he can cut the cord and then the nurses start to take care of you. I am still up on my elbows watching everything. Two nurses, one doctor, a new baby and I are all squished into this little room. Soon after that, the nurses whisk you out of the room and Dr. Weiner finishes up what he is doing and all the time he is saying, "Everything is OK, everything is OK."

Then I am taken back to the main room where all of the other women are who have given birth.

I am the youngster among the women. And the story of what happened is already there.

Everybody is talking about it, including the nurses. That is when I figure out that this was not an ordinary, normal birthing.

I was even more confused. But confused or not, I was exhausted and I slept. And then somebody woke me up and said "Here is your baby."

This was the first time that I really saw you. Up until that moment you had been an idea, a concept. But not real. But now there you were. And you were the most incredible thing I had ever seen. Tiny, fragile, beautiful, calm, serene.

All around me the other mothers were holding screaming, squalling, red-faced, angry little beings, but I was holding a tiny little bundle that was staring up into my face as I was staring into hers and it hit me that I was a mother. And that this gorgeous, precious babe was mine. I was going to be responsible for her.

I was overwhelmed and flooded with more emotions than I had ever experienced in my life. This was real. Not some idea of a baby found in books or movies. This was my real, breathing, dependent baby.

This is a love affair that has never waned. I have not been the perfect mother but I have given it all I had for all of these years. I really did not have a clue how to be a mother. But I was going to do the best I could. I am flawed, impatient, and bullheaded but look how great you have turned out!

I spent the next two years turning to the Dr. Spock Baby Book in order to know what to do. I picked the brains of every other mother that I knew and asked what they would do for each stage of your changing and growing during that first year.

But as luck would have it, you were the perfect baby. You slept all night. You did not have any bottle problems. Your teething went smoothly without problems. You toilet trained early. You had only a few, normal childhood illnesses. You were never a cranky, colicky baby. You rarely cried unless there was a real problem. You did not throw tantrums. You hit all the benchmarks that were in the Dr. Spock book right on time.

So here's to you, the perfect baby. And you have just kept getting better.

Happy Birthday and may there be many, many, many more. You are my great joy."

Mora took a deep bow, the group gave her a rousing bust of applause, and she plopped back down on her floor pillows.

Lex said, "Well, I have not said anything yet, not even to Glory but here is a letter I just sent to Hunter. I kept a copy so that I can remind myself why I don't want to go back and start the mess all over. It will be clear that it is a story in a letter."

My Dearest Hunter:

What has happened to us is shattering.

I am not angry or bitter. Just sad. Our parting was so abrupt, so inconclusive, so devastating.

I have said to you so many times that love is the ultimate commitment. It does risk pain. I took that risk. I gave myself with no subtlety or deviousness. If I must suffer now for that, then it was worth it.

I might have gone to my grave not knowing that I could love so deeply for the second time, and that I could be so happy sharing those feelings with another human being. I am indebted to you for so much.

For making me feel again. For the warm hours that we shared. For the fun times and the times that you did remove your layers of hurt and negative feeling. You showed me the real man under the hard shell. You were my living turtle.

Others saw the shell; I saw the living, breathing being under it all.

I was mistakenly convinced that I could bring that man out into the open. I thought with love and nurturing that I could make you want to make an honest and total commitment. I was wrong.

Whatever you needed from me; assurance of self, or a link to reality, a partner in your charade, I do not after all this time know what it was. What *did* you need from me?

I gave freely. But it is so hard to give when it is not possible to know what your partner wants from you.

I have been very fortunate that I had such a wonderful relationship with Harvey. But it was different. I can't explain how. I was a different person then.

I went into this relationship with no expectations of recreating what I had with Harvey. I don't think any relationship is the same as any other relationship. The ingredients are different and they mix differently.

I knew you were different. I wanted a new relationship based on the people that we are. So I gave self.. I wanted the same from you. I loved you. Over the top. As I said to you, too many times, that I will always love you. But my self-pride has finally kicked in and I need to step back.

I have had independence, and emotional security too long to let myself get into a bad relationship. I can only accept a mutual relationship based on love, respect and commitment. I cannot accept less and still have pride in an "us".

Every fight and every rejection has flattened something. How little effort would have taken from you to be able to put Humpty-Dumpty back together again.

You will not let me bring light into your darkness. Maybe that was never possible.

We had part of it for a while. I guess we lost even that part. You withheld the most important gift that you could have given me. Your real self. And you could not give both of us the one thing that a relationship needed to survive and be strong. Truth!

You have accused me of wanting to create the past. No, that is not true. I just wanted to have a relationship based on love, respect, and integrity. I cannot accept less than that. I was not trying to recreate my relationship with Harvey. I just did not believe that I had to accept less than those essential qualities. Hard to explain and harder to make you see that it is what a woman wants in any man.

I am a grown woman who looked at you with wonder in my eyes. You are not a king or magician but a man, troubled, flawed, conflicted and perhaps a little mad but in many ways wonderful.

I say this with love. I was prepared to accept the man I saw if given an equal chance for a relationship. But you were not willing to reciprocate and accept the troubled, flawed and conflicted woman that you said that you loved.

This is not a plea for a new beginning. After last week we both know that this is not possible. This is a statement of regret of what might have been. I feel great sorrow. For me, for you, and for all of that that will never be. Perhaps never was. Maybe I have deluded myself from the beginning and all that we ever had was just an illusion.

I will survive. You will survive.

Somewhere out there may be partners for us that are not so toxic.

Or maybe there is no partner for me. That is fine too.

I think that my greatest realization is that I don't have to be connected so someone else to provide "happiness" or make me "completed" or "better" or anything. A relationship is only needed for sharing but not for completing. I know, it all sounds too simplistic but I will just leave it at that.

We had it. We lost it. I, too, am guilty. I kept the relationship going long after it had died.

Once I wooded you back with letters and pleas. Now I let you go. There will be no more letters. No more pleas.

Had I fought for you again and had I wept, would you have returned and loved me? We will never know. I will never know.

We are both free now. Free to make new lives that do not include each other.

Our dreams meshed, crossed and now have gone their separate ways. I will try to remember the good and forget the bad.

I truly hope you find great happiness. Most of all I wish you peace from your demons.

Was being with you for these years worth the price that I pay now?

It was. It was.

Alexandria

This brought on a new round of hugs and comments about Lex
and Hunter.

Lex shrugged and said well, I guess I am at a new place. Let's
move this forward. *Hunter topic, closed.* Hey, it is my party. Let's
lighten it up a bit. I have loved what you guys have shared. But let's
just vary the pace a bit. Just like we would do in class."

This got a burst of applause from the Homies.

"OK, Miss Smarty Britches, you pick the next topic."

Lex looked thoughtful and then sported a big evil grin
and looked straight at me and announced, "I pick we each tell
our most embarrassing moment. And boy, do I have a doozy!
But I am not starting, so there, Ms. Law and Order. with all
the rules."

JJ, giving Reg a wink, "We know we can't do this with
out organization and rules, otherwise we are just some sad
group of academics doing a pathetic version of The View. So
tell us, Wise Grand Pu Bah, what is the acceptable order for
us?" This of course brought on an onslaught of laughter from
the group.

I narrowed my eyes trying to work up a glare for the
group but failed miserably. Funny is funny. And I know, I am
the control freak in the bunch.

"Oh, just figure it out for yourselves!" and I flounced myself out to the kitchen for a Diet Coke.

"Well, let's just go the way we are sitting." JJ interjected. Seemed like a plan.

Reggie laughed, "Fine, I'll be the bigger woman and tell mine. Oh, well that line has a whole second meaning, doesn't it? Guess it is true both ways. Hell, who cares."

She continued, "You all know, I married at nineteen. Sorta had to, remember?"

Married that big strong football hero who turned out to be the weak, sniveling, jerk-wad of a husband. Well, I had to go to the free clinic for my first visit to find out if I was preggers. Jerry, ever the gentleman, drove me there, didn't even park, said, 'I'll come back for you in an hour. Just wait outside.'

So much for chivalry . I went in, a scared little teenager, not sure what to do.

The only thing they had told me when I made the appointment was that I had to bring a "specimen" UGH! So I looked for something to put it in. The smallest thing I had was a maraschino cherry jar. I emptied it (eating all the cherries, of course) and then washed, boiled it, thinking that would sterilize it and then filled it. Double eeouee! I then wrapped it in tinfoil. Well, that was going to disguise what it was, right?

So I get out of the car, clutching my "specimen", barely slam the door before my knight in tarnished amour takes off and I proceed to walk up the steps to the clinic.

Somebody is walking out of the open door and I try to scramble in. I manage to hit the raised door-flashing.on the bottom and I go flying. My tin-foiled, little, cherry jar goes one way and I go another. Glass jar meets hard tile floor, right in between the legs of a guy who did have the guts to accompany his knocked-up partner.

"Bedlam ensues. Two people are picking me up. Somebody comes from the back to clean up broken glass, shinny wrapper and the liquid contents. I am crying from embarrassment, somebody is patting my back and I am babbling, "Now I can't see the doctor and I have to find out today! Sad story end, I did see the doctor. I was preggers, got married a month later in my parents back yard.

Sad parents, even sadder groom, smirking guests and a baby six months later. Divorced two years later after another kid. Bad marriage. But the kids are the love of my life. They were and are the best thing I have ever done. Georgie bowed, to keep from making eye contact, Mara stood up and bear-hugged her and the rest of us could not decide whether to laugh or cry.

Then Lex started laughing and the rest of us joined in. And we all could picture this sad, funny tableau. Reggie tripping, little disguised jar flying and the startled look on the dad-to-be as it plops between his feet. And every one of us silently wished that Jerry would suffer a horrible, painful catastrophe between his aging legs.

Mora said, "OK, I'm up. This one is about husbands one and two. This is going to take a while, so get comfy. Some of you know the back story and for a couple of you its new info. So, I have to back up."

I graduated in the top 5%. I had a full ride to Penn State. I was really looking forward to going away to school.

That summer, I went to a cousin's wedding. Same old story. OLD story. Met Bill. Whirlwind courtship. Thought I was Cinderella and he was Prince Charming. He agreed to move to Pennsylvania and I could go to school.

I don't think the ink was dry on the marriage certificate when the plan changed.

Didn't take long to discover he was a mega bastard. World class abuser, physical and worse, mental crap up the old kazoo. The final straw was when he had a sad little affair with, who else? A little bimbo he met in a strip club. How cliché is that?

Don't you love it? What was really funny was he told me one time that the next time he picked a woman it would be for boobs not brains. I love irony. She was married to an abuser too. I guess one woman's abuser is another woman's savior. Some savior.

The abuse had started when we had only been married for about six months. I should have bolted then. But I was filled with that crap that convinces us that if we love him enough and do the right things, he will discover one day what a treasure he has and become the perfect husband.

So I sewed, I baked, I cleaned my little brains out and I had two kids.

Oh, I was the perfect mother. Really. And the entire time, I walked around with that knot in my stomach, wondering when the ugly shoe would drop. It dropped frequently."

"You know what's sad?   All abused wives know exactly what I am talking about, and everybody else say things like,

'Why didn't you leave?',

'Well, that could never happen to me.'

'You have such a strong personality, I can't understand why you didn't just stand up for yourself'. And my personal favorite,

'Why didn't you tell somebody?'   Gosh Glory, we seem to be telling the same story.   I have a feeling that it is the same story for thousands of our sisters, with just variations in time, place and incidental facts. Example?

The one time I went to the police station, bruised ribs and a knot on my head, the burly policeman who took the information said, "Well, Honey, what did you do to get your man all riled up?'

The old handwriting on the wall.   I tucked my tail behind me and slunk home."

I didn't even leave when I found out about the affair.   He made such promises about how everything was going to be so much better. He would become the perfect father, husband, a regular 'father knows best'.   And I bought it. So typical.

My God, same damn story with just different facts.   Yes, somebody needs to do a study.   Why do we stay, why do we hide the abuse, why, why, why everything?

We have already had the worst and we want that wonderful promised fairytale life that we are promised when we are those starry eyed teens. We keep buying the myth over and over again."

"So I spend another chunk of my life in *empty promise Hell*.

Mora paused, looked at us and said, "I know, where is the funny, part?   Well, I told you, it's a long and convoluted road!"

I stayed for almost another two years. Then he did something that was spectacular, even for him.

I was working at Sears. Another stupid story. Any way, I had gotten a raise, and I did not tell Bill. I had started a new bank account. I took that extra money and added it to my little bank account, and deposited my regular check into his account. Oh, yeah, that is one of the things that is common for these controller, abuser types. They control all the money as well as the control of their women.

So one lovely day, I decided to spring my great surprise and he will be so pleased and things will be so hearts and flowers. Well, obviously I had not been paying attention for the past eight years. I told Bill I had this little nest egg.

Gee, Glory, any more of this sound familiar?

So I present my wonderful idea. Let's buy a house. Stop renting. It will be a new start for us. I have been looking and have found places that we could afford in Nanuet and

Hillcrest. We can look further up state if that is what you want.

Bill's response? *'You have how much money?* Did you really think I would want to buy a house? You know I want to move out of New York. I want to go out west. I want to start a bike shop. Don't you ever listen to me?'

He made me write a check to him for the entire amount in my savings.

He slammed out of the house and did not come back for two days. Then he roared up with a new, completely tricked out Harley.

I don't even know how much it was. I tried to find out. The closest I could come was that it was over $20,000. My little nest egg of over $7,000 sucked into that horrible hunk of metal. Years of putting money into that account, and my dreams of a home evaporated into the exhaust fumes from that piece of macho junk.

So, that was my wake up call. I made the decision to leave when that bike came into our carport. Clearly, it told me that the kids and I had no place in his life, his future. We did not want the same things.

I had been enduring an empty existence based on something that did not exist. Smoke and mirrors.

It took me three months to get out. I had to borrow and beg. But, I found a house that I could afford and the kids and I moved. I expected the kids to have issues but they didn't.

Later it occurred to me that when he was at home the kids were as afraid as I was and that it was better for them as well once we were out of his wrath.

Months passed, and things really started getting better. I found I could go to school days if I took the evening shift at Sears. Started out with three classes and then my supervisor let me work out a crazy schedule. Worked a double shift on Friday, Saturday and Sunday. That really freed up going to school. I got through in three years from that lucky break and a kind boss. Got the job at the college and I have never looked back.

Now to the part where I met Terry.

I don't know if it was fate or irony, but my life was to change while I was still going to school.

I had a co-worker that had become a good friend. One day right after I had left Bill, he had really topped himself in the jerk department. We had gone to the lawyer to work on child support. The lawyer had asked him about medical and dental support. Bill pitched a fit. An all out foaming at the mouth, tantrum of the first order. He refused to pay anything. And a miniscule amount of child support. And I agreed to all of it, just to get it over with.

During a coffee break with my boss, she asked me what was wrong. It didn't take much sympathy to get me to spill my sad little beans."

"After her appropriate responses of "What a bastard!" and "I can't believe he could do that" and other sympathetic comments, she invited me to go with her to a party that she was attending. She was dating a dentist and it was some kind of conference at the Rockland Convention Center.

I protested half-heartedly because, damn-it, I was feeling pretty sorry for myself. I told her I could not leave the kids. She said we would have the kids do a sleep-over with her kids, use the same babysitter and all would be hunky dunky. I went.

This was my first time out in over eight years. I had never gone out without Bill. Or the kids. Or even out very much. Eight years of staying home, being Little-Miss-Perfect-Homemaker-Mother. I had been mother at home, reliable employee at work and just recently, student. Up until now, my life had been Brownies, Girl Scouts, school activities for the kids, wife, mother and little robot. I had no other life.

You know, that marriage had been dead in the water for a long time. I just hadn't known it. Suddenly, bang, right square between the eyes. I realized I could be what ever I was willing to work for and wanted to be.

I had begun a new life. A life that no longer included Bill.

For the first time in years, I wanted to go out. That night was my Bastille night. I was liberated.

I was beginning to be a person again.

Now it gets to the weird part. Yeah, it gets weird. I went with Peggy to the party. I even had to borrow a dress. I did not own anything that was not for work, school or to do housework in. Long story short. Yes, JJ, I know that boat sailed! So the story is not so short.

JJ said, "No, I'm liking this boat, I never knew your story."

Well, this is right out of a bad soap opera. That's the night I met Terry. He was one of the attendees. An oral surgeon.

Peggy and her beau, can't remember his name, were dancing and I was sitting at the table thinking how odd it was for me to be there, a voice behind me asks if I want to dance. I automatically said, 'No', but as I turn around and I got to where I could see a face that went with the voice, I was a goner. He was an Adonis. A Lancelot, a tall George Clooney. I added 'problem' to my original no' and we were on the dance floor before he or I could change our minds.

It took six months before I began to accept that I had feelings for Terry. I am just a slow learner.

And Bill just ran true to form. Guess we all know a leopard does not change its spots and all the other adages you can think of. All true.

Then it took another year to get divorced. As soon as Bill found out about Terry, he did everything he could to hold up the paperwork and throw a monkey wrench into the process.

Its not even worth listing his spiteful shenanigans. But lucky for me he did decide to take his hog and himself and move to California. What little child support he had been paying, stopped. One of the few times that his behavior was good for me as well as self serving for him.

Sadly, that worked for me but not so well for the kids. He did not have anything to do with them. Nothing. Of course that hurt them deeply. As they grew older it became harder for them to accept the rejection.

They wanted me to try to find him. I tried. Even used his social security number. I finally had to get a lawyer to track him. I found him in Washington State, remarried, four kids and no interest in his first two. Over the years, they have blamed me. I guess it was easier that just having to accept that he did not give a damn.

And that, My Dears, has created an whole new kettle of fish. Another story for another time. Too long a story for tonight. Glory, we should take our stories on the road as a duo! I really wonder how many women are enduring what I am beginning to see as a syndrome. Women caught in that age old story of a marriage gone bad and the kids blame the mother because she was the one to finally end it.

So back to Terry.

Terry was and is a great guy. Unfortunately, we did not wait long enough to marry and I felt smothered. I kept waiting for the shoe to drop because I had lost faith in men, in relationships and in the whole idea of love. It had me as nuts as when there really was a problem. I had no real way to deal with problems in a marriage. I saw every little thing as a rejection of me.

But I am getting ahead of the story. I need to tell Terry's story to get to the one I am trying to tell.

"Terry had married a nice Long Island girl, they had gone together since high school. He got his degree, she got the baby. He had been a pilot in the AF and when he got out he went into the reserves. He flew every other week end. One weekend, he had gone to his assignment only to find out it was canceled. He drove the three hours to get back home.

Usually he would call if he were coming home but this time he did not, for what ever reason. He arrived home to find his sister's husband's car in his driveway. That would not have been unusual except that it was 2:30 in the morning and his house was dark."

"Kiddies, can you guess the next part of this story? Right! Little wifey-poo is beddy-bye with dear brother-in-law, Carl. Another fine mess.

Well, Terry is extremely practical. Big house, only one kid. So Terry tells soon-to-be-divorced-wife, that they will stay in the same house until the court divides all the assets. He turns the top floor into a bachelor pad of sorts and they continue on. Only person to know about the episode is Terry's sister. And sister and hubby work out their own situation and nobody is the wiser.

Until Terry does something foolish and tells dear wifey that he has met somebody and is thinking about getting married again and wants to proceed with a divorce. Now wifey has the upper hand. Nobody knows about the wife's little escapade and now Terry is the bad guy. Being the good guy that he really is, he takes all the blame for everything.

The daughter, a thirteen year old "only child" thinks he is Attila the Hun, and Terry's sixty-year-old mother is beside herself. He son has done everybody wrong. And the worst part is that nobody tells her anything. So she has no clue why Terry has divorced Barbara.

Well, that was a long road to get to this part of the story. Now we get to an embarrassing part.

Terry and I marry. His mother's name for me? *'The Other Woman'*, she never spoke to me or about me by using my name. Three holidays come around and he goes to his mother's house, his ex is there and my kids and I are persona non grata!

I finally have enough.

The second Thanksgiving is coming up. I tell Terry there is no damn way he is going to his mother's. They are going to come to our house. Terry, being caught between two evils, agrees reluctantly. Very reluctantly.

So, now I finally am preparing for a Thanksgiving with Terry, his mother, uncle, his sister, Vanna, and her hubby, his daughter, two couples we were friends with, and my two kids.

I think it is a nice little grouping. I am convinced that this event will change everything. My new mother-in-law will see that I am a good mother, terrific house keeper, pretty fair cook and all will just be beer and skittles from now on. Boy, was I delusional !

I spent weeks preparing. The family of my beloved is coming to our house. My cooking has to be perfect, the house has to gleam, my children have to be angels.

The big day arrives. Mountains of food cooked to perfection. The golden bird graces a table set with gleaming linen, and my best china and crystal. We are all seated and enjoying our meal.

Well, at least I thought so. Terry is in a cold sweat just hoping for the best. It is almost time for my famous pies. I make a mean lemon meringue and all of the rest of the appropriate holiday pie selections. I am in the kitchen slicing away, and I hear Mommy-in-law-dearest saying to the Uncle, 'Well, I hope *THAT WOMAN* is satisfied, dragging me out to this horrible place with these horrible people. Poor Barbara, home all alone.'

Did she think nobody could hear her? Didn't know and I didn't care. I charged into the dinning room, crashing into the table, knocking over some of my good crystal.

I am seeing red and I am sure with eyes bugging out of my head, I must have looked like Medusa. Words are spewing out of my mouth, I have absolutely no control over what I am saying. Three years worth of frustration, and probably a little residue from the first failed marriage thrown in for good measure. I see Terry look stricken and let out a huge sigh. And I keep going. All of it. I told the dear old lady about Barbara and her late night gentleman caller, Carl.

Now Terry's sister, Vanna, is the one looking stricken. Because of course, she had never told her mother about Carl's late night tryst with Barbara. Of course this is all spanking-bran-new news for the old lady. The uncle just looks amused. Boy, do I know how to break up a party? The house emptied in about five minutes. Including Terry. He goes to his favorite Irish Pub and ties one on. Later, somebody kindly shipped him home in a cab.

Of course, nothing got fixed. His mother still thought I was the woman from Hell. But at least I didn't wreck things for Vanna. She told me not to worry, she was glad it was out, she was tired of keeping it secret.

She and Carl decided to adopt, something she had been trying to get him to agree to for years. As it turns out, that was a good thing and they have been great parents.

Happy ending? Not so much. His mother never spoke to me again and that along with other problems, drove a wedge that we were never able to repair. The irony? After our divorce we have become friends and have been for over twenty years. I think we would have remarried but when he would be available I was involved and vise-versa.

But one more embarrassing part. Sorta. But the embarrassment was not on my part this time. A few months after this memorable Thanksgiving Feast of Horrors, Terry's uncle went into the Bethpage Hospital. We had not known at Thanksgiving that he already been diagnosed with throat cancer.

I had agreed to go with Terry to visit him. At the last minute, Terry said that he would be running late, and he would meet me there. I talked Shanna, a friend, into going with me. We got to the hospital and no Terry.

Here is where I have to describe the scene. I was looking good that day. I have on my new. white linen suit, black, silk blouse, my hair, in all its 70s *bouffantness*, is perfect and I must admit I was feeling like the poor man's

Farah! Just one of those days when it all came together. Lucky for me.

We are waiting in the reception area and there are about ten other people. We are seating next to two very *Long Island Ladies*, extreme poufy hair, revealing clothes, deep décolletage and big hunky jewelry. Enough gold to ransom a kidnapped poodle. They are discussing a horrible bitch that has stolen away the poor schnook of a husband from poor, pure Barbara. Poor, poor Barbara. Poor little Gina.

The flat nasal voice is stating loudly and clearly enough to be heard in Manhattan, 'And have you seen *The Other Woman*? I hear she is as ugly as a mud fence. Flat as a board. But, Boy, she must be something in the sack! Otherwise, why would Terry leave Barbara?'

Just then, Terry comes walking up, I stand up, he kisses me, turns to the two lovelies and says, "Hello, Tina, Hello Janelle, thanks for coming to see Uncle Lou."

I loved the look on the two, heavily made-up faces. They look at me with wide, mascara clumped eyes and I just shrug, turn and follow Terry up to see Unk. One of the good things was that I never saw the little Long Island, tarty cousins again. But I sure would like to have been a fly on the window of their car going home. That would have been a fun conversation to have heard.

This got a round of applause. Mora knew how to tell a story.

Reggie said, "OK, I have a quick one. I don't even need to get up for it."

MONKEY BUSINESS

I was ten years old. My mother had a really strange sister. We used to go over to her house, well, to a trailer really, and have dinner once a month, on a Thursday. Sometimes my dad went and sometimes he didn't. He hated to go there.

Aunt Mazie. Dad called her Crazy Mazie. She had parakeets and a monkey. A rhesus monkey. Nasty little thing. And the birds used to fly free.

Aunt Mazie couldn't cook worth a darn and even if she could Dad would tell me to eat as little as possible and he would stop and get Mexican food for us on the way home. He said her food was contaminated by the birds and worse yet by the stupid monkey. The monkey's name was Sampson.

So this particular Thursday, we are all there for a forced monthly dinner, and right in the middle, the ugly. little monster hops on my head and proceeds to pee. Dad can't pry Sampson off because it has its claws digging into my French braids. Dad's pulling, the monkey is digging, stuff is dripping down my hair and onto my clothes and everybody is screaming.

Aunt Mazie is howling, 'Don't hurt Sampson!" My dad is yelling, 'I'll kill the damn thing'. And my mother is just yelling. I'm crying. Finally the monkey lets go. My dad shoves my head under the kitchen sink faucet, rinses me out like a dirty sock, pulls me out from under the running water, hands me a dishtowel and says to my mom, 'I think it is time to go now.'

Well, that was our last dinner there. I never saw that damn monkey again.

Reg finished this little monkey tale and everybody was in major hysterics. Les was laughing so hard she was hiccupping.

Gorgie and JJ said, "Never saw that monkey again!" at the same time. "Oh My God!"

"That is the best story of the monkey topic, also the only one!" Lex finally squeaked out. "I hate monkeys. Hate 'em. But I never had one pee on me." She started laughing and hiccupping again.

JJ said, "Gee, Want to go to the Bronx Zoo next week? I'll bet we could find some cousins." Reg threw a shoe at her.

Regina stood up retrieved her shoe and said with as much dignity as she could muster, "I think we all need a potty break and I need to walk around for a bit."

9:55

We all did what we needed to do, I replenished the ice bucket, added dip, chips and other munchies, Lex carted everything into the living room. JJ and Regina lugged dirty glasses to the kitchen, loaded them into the dishwasher and got out clean glasses. Mora got out the room spray and spritzed everything until the rest of us yelled for her to stop.

We all trouped back into the living room. Everybody gravitated back to their own self assigned places and looked expectantly at me.

Does anybody realize that we are now in a weekend mode? We have been reveling for over twelve hours. I am having fun and can keep going, but how do the rest of you feel?

One by one the rest of the group confirmed to keep the party going. Mora said, "You know, I think we have needed this for a long time. We are in a cleansing mode. You know, kinda like those sweat lodge things that the men do. Only we do it with lots of food and a comfy place to sit. No dummies here!"

JJ said, "I know I am good, even after all these years, we did not all know all of our stories, bits and pieces, but now we are weaving something that is good for all of us. Thanks to Lex, I think this was just the right time. I really believe that this is so good. Sometimes we think that others have the perfect life, or handle problems better, or any of the things that we imagine about how people manage to live better, and then we discover that life is messy, and difficult and nobody gets a free pass. There is no manual on how to live life. Mankind has been doing this kind of story telling since the caves. It's what binds us into a village. So let's just keep going! Anybody need to go home?" She looked at the group and asked, 'Who's good for a few more stories"

And like the school teachers that we all are, we raised our hands in agreement.

I said, "Good, Reggie it is your turn. Regale us!"

She stood up and said, "Okey, Dokey, I have one that continues our themes in two ways. Crappy husbands, and the irritating phone. I've had my own crappy husband and now it is even other people's husbands. I am so tired of jerks. I had a call the other evening. This happened about a week ago. I was all set to have a lovely evening. All my papers were graded and I was just going to veg out with a movie I had been trying to get time to watch. Dog in lap, munchies in handy reach, cokes at the ready, the credits are rollin' and ….."

A Ma Bell Nightmare

A shrill scream split the luscious solitude of my evening. It was Ma Bell in all of her wondrous glory. By the way, when did Alexander Graham Bell turn into a woman? Just wondering.

One of my problems is that I wonder about these things. Isn't a mother figure supposed to soothe? I have found that answering the phone does usually the opposite. I figured this call would not add to my peace of mind this evening either.

Anyway I pickup of the offending piece of cold plastic and before I could even answer in my usual, cheery 'Whadda want?' this Long Island nasal voice asked, 'Did I do something to offend you? Did you forget my number or do you have a new love? Which one is it, Reg?'

Quickly running down my list of friends, enemies, co-teachers and odd acquaintances and even some old boyfriends, I could mentally picture several who might be or might be attached to this irritating voice. So I brilliantly came up with a sparkling question of my own, "No, what makes you ask?'

So, they can all be gems! I was trying to think fast and figure out how to get rid of this intrusion of my otherwise quiet (O.K. insert boring here) evening. Even boring would have proven better than talking to this voice.

The voice continued, 'Well, you moved several months ago and I have not had an invite to see your new place! Jack said he saw it and it was terrific!'

Ah ha! Jack! A clue. I knew six Jacks if you counted the butcher. But the butcher was not one of my usual visitors. That left five. Which one of them had to live with this voice?

The voice was continuing and I was not listening to the words as much as I was hearing the sound of a subway coming to a screeching stop. Oh, I digress again. Imagine having to listen to that all day.

I tried to focus on the words. I tuned back in the middle of her continuing prattle.

'and did you know that I am in decorating school now? It is just so divine. I will be able to save so much money when I do my own decorating and I just know that once people see my place they will want me to do theirs.'

'You might even want to have me do you, because you know what your last place was like. Oh, Reg, I didn't mean to insult but you know you just don't have that special eye, now do you?'

Oh, God, what do I have to do to get this voice to stop. O.K. Get another clue and then I can say something brilliant and get off this auditory train wreck.

"So, what else is new?' A voice like this was going to tell all and I could get a fix on *who*. Then I could say something clever and get the Hell off.

'Did anyone tell you that we just went to Italy? It was just glorious!'

Oh, great, that could be any of the other five Jack's wives, girlfriend, or their whatevers.

But before I could ask another missile seeking question, she continued, "and Natash just made cheerleader in her freshman year, can you believe it?"

Bingo! Even with my large circle of "Jacks" friend and foe, there was only one that I knew of with a daughter, Natasha. Jack Elgin. Damn! This was not my pick for conversation of the evening. Not even close. I had managed to drop this trio off my radar. I was not interested in a conversation with or about any of the three.

But I jumped in thinking maybe I could ward off spending my entire evening listening to her go on about this endless listing of family accomplishments. I have had some endless conversations with Rosalie in the past and I was hoping to keep this whole issue in my definite past.

The lovely Jack that was married to the owner of this voice was my nightmare. I have spent the last two years with this jerk popping up everywhere, Where I live, at school, at parties, when even sometimes when I'm grabbing a coffee, but I thought I had it under control. I thought I had gotten rid of this nasty stalker.

Three months ago I had just had it. I told him that if he showed up one more time, I would go to the police and then to his wife. He seemed to have been sufficiently concerned that I would do that and fortunately for me this was enough, I hoped, to get him away from me. I had not seen him since.

Now surprise, surprise, I have wifey-poo on the phone and I have to get her off and end it forever.

But I couldn't come up with anything that would do the trick.

I told her that I was working on my PHD and I was drowning in work and after I got it finished I would get back together with her and we would catch up.

I know, I am a sniveling coward. So if any of you can help me out here, I am open to suggestions. I know that there is another phone call in my near future. I got rid of him, now I have to get rid of good old Rosalie.

Lex said, "You know, all of us have been there. I wish I could get an extra step on my school pay for each time I have had to dance around somebody else's mess of a husband. Years ago when Harvey was still alive, we lived next-door to a couple and their four kids."

Kirk was one of those larger than life characters and Lynette was Miss Mousy. Oddly she was tall, muscular and imposing. So her personality did not go with the way she looked.

Now that I am older and somewhat wiser, I can guess what some of the story was. I learned a little of it later.

He was one of those jerks that is always trying to get women alone. He had trapped me a couple of times in the kitchen at house parties. So I became very careful not to get myself in the situations where he could do that. One weekend, Harv had gone to play golf so his car was not in the driveway.

The door bell rang, I could see Kirk on the other side, as I got to the door, he boomed out, 'Hey, Lexie Girl, it is your lucky day. I have come to take you to lunch, so grab your stuff and let's boogie.'

I must have gapped at him. Because he started to repeat himself. I finally found my voice and I said, 'Kirk, take your sorry butt home and go tend to your wife. Why she wants you. I don't know, but you ought to be down on your knees, thanking her that she does.' And I slammed the door on his pathetic face.

That night, I told Harv what happened and asked him if I should tell Lyn. He said, 'What are you going to tell her? She will find an excuse for it and then you can never be her friend again, and she is going to need you as a friend. That is for sure.'

Harv was so wise.

A couple of months later, Lyn's father died and she inherited a little over 80K, and a little after that, Kirk walked out the door, got a little twenty-something and shacked up.

I thought, well, at least Lyn has money to help her start over.

Surprise! I did not realize just how low Kirk could go. He went to court and his lawyer managed to get him half of Lyn's inheritance. I was stunned.

She moved up to Geneva, went to school and became a researcher. Her kids never spoke to their father until he had a car accident with the Corvette that he bought from his spoils, the new wife disappeared and Lyn wound up caring for him until he died a few months later.

I was pretty sheltered then between my own childhood and Harvey. But in the past years, I have become very educated by what people can do to each other.

I have just seen a very sad case with one of my students with her boyfriend. They had only been together since the beginning of the semester, and the boyfriend shot her. They met in my Brit Lit class.

I know all of you know about it. What you don't know is that her mother has been to see me three times. She wants me to give her answers. And I don't have any. The poor woman.

I added, "You know, I have been thinking about that lately. Over the years, I have come to feel lucky that many of the women I have known have not had more serious problems. You can't go a week without two or three stories in the news about a woman who has been stalked to death. We have not really come that far from the caves and the idea of women being something owned or possessed.

JJ looked at me sadly, "Yes. We could spend a week talking about it, and you know what is really sad? We would not change one thing. In the past several years, I have tried to talk to several students who were being abused, stalked, smothered, and every damn time, the girl told me to go pound sand. They just don't get it until it is too late most of the time. Have you seen the statistics on how many girls have been abused by the time they are twenty-one? It is staggering."

Suddenly, all eyes were on Georgie. She is our quiet one. She is our sane one who is very reserved and private. Tears were streaming down her face and both JJ and Reg had scooted over to put their arms around her.

JJ looked back at me with a slight shrug, I shrugged back. I didn't have a clue. Reg was patting Georgie and saying, "What's the matter. Was it something one of us said?" Georgie kept shaking her head, no. Finally, after a few minutes Georgie as able to talk.

"You know I have sat and listened to your stories for years. Especially tonight hearing Glory and Mora. I know what they are saying about shame. I have never been able to talk about my marriage. I know you all know that my husband divorced me. What you already know is that it was a nasty divorce.

Brad got his secretary pregnant, left me, left the two boys, and now they are this happy little family. But the real story is so much worse. So out of our little band of BFFs, there are really three of us who have been one of the women who have been controlled and vilified and beaten down mentally. Brad didn't beat me physically. That's not his style. His way was to make sure that all of those around him become so demoralized and so dehumanized that we could not function out of his control.

Georgie let out a long shuddering sigh. "Are you sure you want to hear this? It is a long one. I don't know how to tell it except to go all the way back to the beginning. And I have never talked about it to anybody. Ever. Glory and Mora are right. I do feel guilty. There had to be something wrong with me. I still believe that. Yes, I know I am supposed to know better. I even spent years with a therapist. But I never told her the real story either. I just couldn't. So I guess I wasted a lot of time and even more money" She gave us a weak smile. "Guess I should have saved all that money and just talked to you guys!"

Reg patted her hand. "Sweetie Pie, you can tell us the story or not. That is up to you. But you know, it has helped all of us to talk. God knows, we can't shut up. That's our style. But I know it works for me. I kept family secrets for a long time and they just ate away at me. They festered. I really got tired of being a martyr and keeping my mouth shut. They crap on us and we are supposed to just shut up and protect their reputations. That's a lot of bull. And I did the therapy thing too. That worked because I needed somebody outside of my problems to help me be objective. So, Honey, that is up to you."

Georgie has a way of holding herself very still. She is more of a watcher than a participant. She speaks quietly and deliberately. Her passion seems to be reserved for her classes. She is a dynamic teacher with a love for all things British. Her classes fill up quickly and she is very respected by all of our faculty. Over the years we have just accepted that she is the quiet, reserved, proper one in our group.

Taking another deep breath, Georgie began her story.

"I grew up in Montclair New Jersey. Upper middle class. My mother was a family court judge, and my father was a corporate lawyer. I had a privileged childhood. The right schools, the right extra activities, the right contacts. When I said I wanted to be a teacher, you would have thought I had declared that I wanted to be a pole dancer."

A gentle laugh rippled through the group as we all imagined Georgie as a pole dancer.

Well, my father said he would compromise with my "little obsession" as he called it. I would go to Princeton. I could get a teaching degree but he would leave the door open for any change I might want to make in my career aspirations. He thought I would wake up one day and figure out that law was the only real career and that teaching was for those who did not have higher ambitions or abilities.

My father was a grand manipulator. Took me years to understand that. My mother's career was totally directed by him. He made all of the decisions for the family. From choosing how our home was decorated, how it was run, hiring the house help, all the way to what my mother wore to what was prepared for dinner. I have two older brothers. I don't remember them making decisions that went away from what my father wanted. And growing up, I was a good, dutiful daughter. See, the groundwork had already been done for Brad. I was trained to be the perfect wife.

Well, I didn't cave on the teaching which surprised everybody, especially me. I thought I was a real radical. I had broken free from all that oppression. Silly me.

I was still living at home when I got the job at the college. I wanted to move out but every time I tried, my father talked me out of it. One weekend my father asked me to play tennis at the club. I was surprised when another couple joined us. It turned out to be Brad and his sister. Brad was one of the new Junior Lawyers in my father's firm. I was so naive that it was years before I figured out that even that meeting was part of my father's manipulation.

Same story. Brad swept me off my feet. Of course I was convinced that he loved me for me. But it sure turned out to be a fast track for him in the firm. Fast courtship, and within six months I was a new bride.

The verbal abuse was subtle at first. I didn't cook like his mother had. She was a gourmet cook, the ultimate house keeper, raised perfect children and was superior in every way. Every thing I did was compared to her high standard and I never measured up. I chalked it up to the fact that I was still learning and that I hoped that I would get better as time went on. Well, in his eyes, I did not get better. He accused me of not trying, not caring, and he blamed my teaching on my other failures.

My teaching job was the one thing I would not cave on. It was a bone of contention my entire marriage. But really the least of my problems.

The first six months were normal. I really didn't even know what to expect. The model that I had observed at home was with the husband making all the decisions so that is the way I thought it was supposed to be and Brad was definitely in charge.

By the end of that first six months, Brad was coming home less and less. It was always something to do with the law firm. Meeting with clients, going to functions to get new clients, doing what he had to do to get ahead.

I complained once and he told me that because he was one of the partners' son-in-law, he had to work harder than anyone else to prove himself. I accepted it.

When he was home, it was a constant barrage of criticism.

This next part is really hard to talk about. Even our physical life was an area that he criticized.

He found me lacking. He would compare me to the other women he had been with.

I was even surprised that I found myself pregnant toward the end of the first year. Our physical life was dying a slow death and the pregnancy seemed to end it all together.

But that did not stop his constant barrage of comments about my figure. Once he even said, 'You know, most women have a glow about them and look good during pregnancy, but I guess that doesn't apply to you.'

According to my doctor I was in the low range for weight gain but Brad told me I looked like a blimp. We were at dinner once, when he made the comment in front of everyone that he could make money by renting out my backside for car ads. I got to the point where I did not want to go to social functions and of course he ridiculed that by saying that he could understand why I would not want to compete with the other women.

There was nothing positive in the relationship. He never spoke to me except to belittle. He was never home. We would go months without sharing a meal and soon after the baby was born, I began to sleep in the nursery. Eventually I took over the guest room and we had separate bedrooms for the rest of our pathetic sham of a marriage.

I know, you are all asking yourselves how I managed to have another child. Well, I am about to shock you all. I didn't.

Five startled faces stared at Georgie. Not only was this the most she had ever said at one time, and had she shocked us already with facts we had not known, but now she was telling us that she was not Tad's birth mother.

Georgie made a little wan smile and continued, "You know I have a sister. She has never married and she is now a partner in Dad's firm. She is Tad's real mother. Tad does not know. Janelle had him while she was in Law School. She did not want a child. Over the years she has been a good aunt, but she seems to have no regrets about giving him up.

The only reason that Brad agreed to adopt Tad was to please my father, of course. I have worried for years that Brad would let it slip that he was not his father. It has been one of the facts that he uses to manipulate me. He still does. All these years later. The boys never saw much difference in the way he treated both of them. He has never paid much attention to either of them. And when neither wanted to go into law, they seemed to have slipped completely off of his radar. The boys have tried so hard over the years to get his attention.

I learned that nothing I had to say had any interest for him. Not anything to do with my teaching and he certainly did not share any of his life with me. And if I was foolish enough to venture an opinion on anything political or any thing about the larger world, he would just look at me blankly and answer with a one or two word sentence designed to end the conversation. It did.

This sounds so boring. Even as I am telling you all of this I sound whinny even to me. There is just no way to make anybody understand who has not lived it. How it feels to live with somebody who makes it clear that they do not like you much less do not love you. That you mean less to them than the person who waits on them in a restaurant or cleans the room in a hotel.

The harder I tried, the worse I was treated. But from the outside looking in, I had everything. A beautiful home, the choice to work or not, an upscale life style, healthy children, and most of all, a handsome, achieving husband. I felt ridiculous every time I complained. Even my mother would tell me I was being foolish. She had lived it and she still couldn't see past the fairytale façade into the empty shell of a life not lived.

That is why this sort of abuse is so horrible. Because humans are not geared to withstand a constant, relentless, daily dose of being told they are worthless. It really does not take that long before there is no self esteem or pride left. And like Glory, I have done a ton of research about this topic. I have done what I can to try to help students. I recognize the abuse syndrome in students very quickly. I try to hook these kids up with some professional help. Sadly I think it comes too late for so many even as young as they are. The scars from this go so deep.

When Brad left it was actually a relief. I will never be the achiever that I think I could have been with a different father and a different marriage. But I do know that I am much better and get better every year.   I have a good relationship but I don't ever want to get married again.

Reg said, "You know, I get it. I do. I had a mad crush on a boy in high school. We were dating, but he treated me as a non person but ridiculed me to his friends right in front of me. I am not comparing my little deal with you. I am just saying that I know how it felt for that short time. I took his crap because he was a big deal and I wanted to be a big deal by being his girlfriend. And he broke up with me. Society empowers men in a way that it does not empower women."

Georgie hugged Reg and said, "You're right. it is the same for many women more than people know or want to know. It is a crapshoot when we get married. Because it's all moonlight and roses until they get that ring on your finger and then the real guy comes shinning through. Sometimes you get the lollipop and sometimes you get the stick.

I know that you all have seen that I am different than I was years ago when we all became friends. I was amazed then that you even wanted me in the group and I am so grateful for your friendship and support. Much of my healing has come because of you. You have been my lifeline.

Now, Glory Girl, let's move on to somebody else. I am pooped."

"Here is a new topic," I said," I have another issue that irritates the bejaberes out of me."

"I have been thinking about why I became a teacher," I began, "I started college with the idea that I would become a lawyer. I was going to change the world by making new law about abused women and children. Ironic, huh? I was not among them then. But I was acutely aware of the abuses I had seen growing up. Especially among some of the ethnic groups. My mother had been a volunteer for a shelter for women and children, so Viv and I had heard and seen many of the real life abused.   And yet it took me years to figure out that I had become one of them.   Go figure."

Nothing changed in my first two years.   At the end of the second year, my English Professor asked me to be his teaching assistant.   I loved the class I had just taken with him so I accepted. Well, that changed the trajectory of my life.

Suddenly I am immersed in James Joyce, Charles Stewart Parnell, Katherine O'Shea for an entire semester. It is a love affair to this day.   My beginning of understanding that history and literature are all tied up in how we perceive the world.   How great literature changes the world.

I feel as if I have changed the world every time I get a class into a discussion about how you have to read about these people and read the books that Joyce wrote to be able to discuss Irish history.   Naturally it is not that simple, but to see that epiphany of understanding that there are pieces to the puzzle of life, history, literature and that if you have giant holes in knowledge, you will have giant holes in your understanding of the world.

I never cease to be amazed at people who think they are educated have so little knowledge of how an issue got from A to Z. They will base all of their thinking on a few facts and then become mired in faulty reasoning. TV thinking.

I don't mean that everybody can know everything. God knows, what I do not know fills libraries. But, if somebody tries to have an opinion about something, it is really helpful to get the facts.

Oh, good grief, I have just expostulated on my main soapbox issue. But I am so tired of people who get an idea about something that is based on either faulty information or faulty reasoning and yet are not capable of listening to new information. That is what education is all about. The ability to absorb information and have ideas that are in constant flux.

JJ grinned and said, "Well, flux you! But I totally agree with you. I don't know which is more tiresome, a student who thinks they already know it, so you can't get them to have a crack that will let new knowledge in, or administration that has the same closed-minded mindset about anything "old". I have spent the last two months trying to get the head of the department to let me change some of the sources for one of my classes."

Lex said, "Speaking of Joyce, I remember my dad talking about "Home Rule". He could really get going. He was a rabid Parnellite. He used to tell me the stories at bedtime. He thought that the love story between Parnell and O'Shea was the greatest love story of all time. I guess I do too. And he knew Joyce so well that he could quote great chunks from all of his books.

It is no wonder that we are all obsessed with Joyce, Chaucer, Shakespeare, Dickens, and hundreds of others that have that history connection.

I was at a dinner party last week and somebody asked me if I taught Steven King. I had to really get under control and not laugh. The "literature deprived" do not take kindly to mockery. Anyway, he really wanted to argue about what a great writer King is.

You all know what is coming.

Groans from the group. And Mora stood up and said, "Please let me finish this. Your lovely, clueless dinner partner said, 'Well obviously, he is a great writer, look how many people buy his books and he is rich.' And if your partner was really on top his game, he looked you right in the eye and said, 'OK, how much do you make?' Give me a buck for every time some jackass has used the same, ignorant argument and I could retire."

Everybody was nodding and shaking their heads sadly. This is a topic that we seem to gravitate to frequently.

Lex continued, "You know, I just read a paper on how reading is declining, and the classics are becoming the purview of only those in academia. I think that is true. How many of you get the students who announce to you proudly, 'Hey, I didn't read a book the entire time I was in high school.' And my personal favorite, 'Why do we have to read this shit, what does it have to do with real life?' And now I have just brought our discussion full circle. The inability of today's public to get the value of literature, history and how it is affecting the fabric of society. I really worry about the future of this country. We are in an instant gratification mode. We have devalued reading and the knowledge of history. Today's kids are all about themselves. "

Georgia said, "Society is always complaining about the Great Unwashed. They need to focus on the Great Unread."

Lex said in her best Irish lilt, "You know, Me Lassies, I wish I could go to the next St. Paddy's parade in the City and ask all of me countrymen who Parnell was, and name one of the Joyce novels."

Mora snorted, "Hell, not one percent could tell you who Joyce was."

JJ said, "I just finished a report for our illustrious leader. It is about why we need to read and why read the classics.

Are we the only ones who are concerned with the fact that 42% of all students will never read another book after college, 80% of all Americans did not buy a single book last year, and 90% of all Americans do not have a working knowledge of basic American History, many of whom have a college degree or two.

I even included five reasons that reading is beneficial because I have the feeling even he does not get it.

1. Improves a person's personal ethics
2. Develops a National identity and world view
3. Cultivates personal wisdom and understanding of human interaction
4. Entertains
5. Improves communication skills

Mora harrumphed, "Well, yeah, did you ever try to communicate with anybody from the math department?" to great hoops from the group.

11:50

Reg, stood up, touched JJ on the arm, and announced, "Potty time! And guess what? I am hungry again. I think it is time for another delivery. What sounds good to everybody? Or should I ask, what is open that is close to here? Does anybody realize that it is almost noon?

Everybody looked expectantly at me. "There's no place that is delivering at this time. If everybody is hungry, the Blue Bird Dinner is just up the road. Who's up for a little road trip?

Five hands went up. So I shrugged, and started looking for my purse. "Two cars? Or do we all want to cram into Reg's Queen Mary of a car?

Everybody raised their hands again. The Buick won. You can take the teacher out of the classroom, but you can't take the classroom out of the teachers.

We all trooped outside, piled into the behemoth car and motored our way to the diner.

If I had expected a scene from Hopper's Night Hawks it was not to be. I don't know why I expected to see an empty diner. I guess because we had been partying for so long, and yet it still felt like the middle of the night instead of the middle of the day that it was. The diner was beginning to fill up for lunch but because it was Saturday, it was still not that full.

We jammed into the round corner booth, picked up the billboard sized menus and began to pick from breakfast to dinner items. That's what I love about diners. Order anything, any time.

Lex lowered her menu and with an evil grin on her face, said "This place is a cross between *Diner* and Five Easy Pieces. OK, who is Jack Nicholson?"

Reg giggled, "Oh, my God, don't look now but it's the same waitress. Look at the helmet hair."

Just then Flo, or whatever her name was, started toward us. Blame it on being up all night or plain silliness, but we all had a laughing fit and almost had it under control, when she looked at us with great distain and said, "What can I getcha?"

We went off. Near hysteria. Six respectable college instructors, dressed in our usual garb which screamed 'teacher' from twenty yards away, and we were having a funny-fit and could not get under control.

Pearl, because that is what her name tag proudly displayed on an ample chest, looked at us for a nano-second, and turned away, saying loudly, "When you ladies are ready, let me know."

Well, we tried, every time we were almost settled, somebody said something and we were off again.   Finally, I starting holding up a shushing finger every time somebody began a new wisecrack, and we were quiet for long enough for Pearl to come back and she pointedly asked, "Do you think you can all manage to order or do ya need more time?"

Reg said, "I want the Blue Bird Special. Everything. A cuppa coffee and a glass of milk."

Around the table we went. You would have thought we were lumberjacks with the amount of food ordered. I had my usual order with my usual Diet Coke. Lex shook her head, and I commented that it was my version of caffeine, and how was her coffee different?

We chatted about school issues while we waited for the much needed nourishment to arrive at our communal table.

When it arrived, we dug in. As usual, our priorities were intact. Eat now, talk later.

Finally, a companionable lull arrived. I looked around to see if our table was needed by waiting patrons. Nobody appeared to need our space. Pearl came to clear and I told her to let me know, if she needed the table. She shot me a grateful look, said she would and left with her first load of emptied plates.

Georgie said, "You know what is really weird? Maybe I should say, something to think about. Somebody mentioned the movie *Diner* earlier. Think about how many buddy movies are made. Tons. And only a handful of the female counterparts. *Steel Magnolias?* Name some more."

"*Terms of Endearment?*" "No," somebody answered, "that was mother-daughter."

"Beaches, Thelma and Louise, Witches of Easwick." The group blurted out the titles.

JJ, our movie buff, said seriously, "Look at what happens in each of these movies. They die, get raped, die from cancer. But look at the male buddy movies. It would take forever to name all of them. All the way back to the early movies. Name a novel that any of us teach that is a female buddy story by or about female bonding."

"How did we get on this topic?" I asked.

"This is huge and we could spend an entire evening talking about it." Lex commented.

The group fell silent. This was another reminder of the status of women.

I looked at Lex and then said to the group. "All of you know that Lex does teacher training for the college right? Well, I don't know if you know about a piece that she does for the newbie's. It is really effective."

"Lex, I know you don't have it with you, but could you just tell it? I wish every teacher could hear it. It really slams home the point that we need to be aware that we do not always know what is going on with students."

All eyes looked at Lex. "Ok, I give the new, adjunct instructors this piece as a handout at the end of the first quarter and ask them to write a response about how they think they affect the classroom mood, tone and student interaction. Then I ask them to write three things they will do in their own classrooms. I revisit the topic at the end of the semester and I even have a question on the final. OK, I will do it verbally but it may be a little off of what is on my handout. I wrote this about ten years ago. The piece is called,"

The Special Space

He sits alone. The din of the idea exchange swirls and rockets around him. But in his space he is protected. He does not know why he needs this special space, he just knows that he needs it.

The teacher is asking a question. Through this special mist, he hears his name. Shivers of panic shoot through his body. His throat constricts with choked off words. He knows that all eyes are focused on him. His own eyes are glittery. He hears the laughter and the tittering. The pretty blonde girl who sits next to him makes a sound that he understands all to well. It is somewhere between disgust and dislike.

Dislike. This is the feeling that he knows best. His mother must have disliked him or else, how could she have left him? Left him with this family that dislikes him so much. They don't like his clothes, his behavior, and most of all they dislike his mother.

They tell him how bad she is. They tell him about the men, the booze, and they tell him things that he really can't understand.   But he does understand that when they are telling them about her they are really telling him that the bad is connected to him.   He doesn't know what he did that was so bad.   But his mother is bad so he must be bad too.

He knows that there is a continual hurt and ache. Sometimes it is so bad that he cannot breathe.   Every minute of every day he hurts. 'Please,' he pleads, 'just let the hurt stop.'

Why can't everybody just leave him alone?   The kids fight with him, tease him, and stare at him with unveiled disgust. They call him names or even worse the reject him when he tries to join in what they are doing. Sometimes they act as if he is not even there.

He is filled with anger. So much anger. But he knows that if he can push first, then maybe the hurt will be less than when they punch him or trip him or call him names.

He wonders why there is not one person who likes him. There is nobody, not the people who have to take care of him, not a teacher and not one single person at school. He is filled with so many emotions. He tries to tell himself that he does not care. He tries to go to that place, deep within him, where he does not feel anything.

He moves slowly to science class. The teacher ignores him. For some reason this is even worse than being yelled at. He begins to kick the chair of the student in front of him. The other student turns quickly and punches him. The teacher finally notices him and gives him detention. Nothing happens to the other student.

He feels the dislike rolling toward him in waves, from the teacher, from the students.

He retreats to his special space. He lets his eyes unfocus. He sees nothing and feels nothing.

He is in his special space.

Reg said, "Lex, I have not heard that before but one of the math teachers was talking about it in the cafeteria. That is so powerful. So short but it says so much about how teachers miss signals, miss opportunities and just plain contribute to the problem. It should be required reading for all teachers.

There should be classes on how to deal with the bullied, the abused, the problem kids. I think we are all guilty of dealing with the behaviors but not the underlying problems."

We kicked around the ideas about teaching and the problems that we find in the classroom. We discussed how so many of the problems are the same at all levels.

JJ said, "You know, this is such a huge topic. And I know it is important, but right now, let's change the subject."

"Hey, I announced to the group. Did I ever tell you about the time, that the dog I had before Hamlet saved my life?" Five pairs of eyes lit up at the prospect of a dog story.

So cleverly, I had changed the topic and had swung into one that everybody was into. Dogs.

"The kids and I were still living in the first house on the Hudson," I began. "Pretty safe neighborhood. There hadn't been that many problems that I had heard about."

Saved by Shakespeare

Both older kids were at an age where they were usually out on weekend nights and the twins were on a sleep-over.

So, I settled in to enjoy my evening. I had given myself the night off and I wasn't going to grade papers, or do anything else that could even resemble work. It was a *me* night.

I was in bed with my bag of pretzels, a tub of cream cheese dip and I was enjoying a vapid Friday Nite Movie.

Shaky, for Shakespeare of course, a standard-sized dachshund, with a head like a Doberman, was under the covers at the end of the bed. Shaky was over forty pounds of muscle and meanness. His personality was closer to a Doberman than it was to a Dachshund. I had complained for years about his aggressive nature.

Little did I know that the mean streak in lil' ole Shaky was going to pay off, big time!

Suddenly, Shaky came roaring out from under the covers, and threw himself at the bedroom door. I got up to let the little bugger out, thinking that he probably heard or smelled a skunk and wanted to exercise his killer instincts.

He flew down the stairs, unusual for him to move that fast, and I am mumbling something about 'if you get skunk sprayed' I am going have to give you the dreaded tomato bath' and just as I hit the bottom stair, there is a huge crash, and the unmistakable sound of breaking glass.

I immediately knew that it was the sliding door off the family room. I ran back up stairs, locked myself back into the bedroom, then I grabbed the cordless and ran to lock myself into the bathroom. Of course I was worried about the dog, the noise! Now I was scared out of my wits. That glass did not break itself and that is what Shaky had been hearing. Somebody removing the sliding door and it had shattered.

I was trying to get my breathing under control. I was hyperventilating so loudly that I could not hear and I needed to hear if anybody was trying to break into the bedroom door.

I was mad at myself for not trying to see where Shaky was. I was muttering, 'Please let him be OK, please Let him be OK.'

Within minutes I could hear the sirens getting closer. I stayed in the bathroom, shrugging my self into the robe on the hook, thinking, irrationally, that it was my ugly, serviceable one, and wondering if I would have time to get a better one out of the closet?

Then I heard banging on the door to the bedroom, and a couple of loud voices, then I heard Shaky, scratching at the door. I came out of the bathroom, and went to open the bedroom door.

I followed the cops back down stairs, and went to see the mess. The glass slider off the family room was in shards at the bottom of the deck. One of the cops was flash-lighting a blood trail that goes all the way back to the fence on the other side of the long, sloping yard. On the other side of our fence was over eight acres of dense, wooded land.

I asked the cop if he thought it had been a burglar. He gives me a funny look and said, 'Yeah'.

I comment that the intruder must have gotten cut when he dropped the slider. The cop looks at me, said, 'Lady, your dog got him. There is no blood on the glass. Look at your dog.'

I bent down to Shaky and saw that he had blood all over his muzzle. He was still quivering and thrumming with anger and fear. I picked him up to calm him, no easy feat because of his considerable poundage.

I started to take him inside, and the cop said, 'Wait, we gotta swab him.'

Well, now I am in an episode of CSI. He says, 'Can you hold him till the tech gets here? But don't touch his mouth.'

I sat down in my chair in the family room, trying to calm him down and we waited a few minutes. A young guy came in with a big square box, opened it, and came over. Shaky starts growling low in his throat, and the kid backs up.

I told the kid to tell me what to do, and he hands me the oversized q-tip thingy. I got Shaky to open up, also no easy feat. He had jaws like a bear trap. The kid wants a swab from the inside, and then several new swabs from the outside of his mouth. Then he very cautiously handed me a gauze square, all the time watching Shaky's barred teeth. Right then, Shaky was not ready to make any new friends. So I rubbed as much blood as I could onto the chunk of gauze.

I get the job done, and kid suggests that I might want to take the dog upstairs while they get the rest of their work done. I get that nobody wants to deal with Killer Dog, and we go upstairs where I get him cleaned up. His body was still a mass of only slightly controlled anger.

Shaky was not thrilled with the Listerine part of the cleanup. Or the tooth brushing. Note to self: get new tooth brush.

The cops were there all night. Scared the older kids silly when they got home.

The next day, the twins were very disappointed that they had missed all of the excitment. And they made a little hero cape for Shakes, that's what the boys call him, out of an old towel, They used markers to write Super Dog.

Weeks later when the little scumbag was caught breaking into another house. This time the little scummer had the misfortune to choose the wrong house. The owner of the house was a cop. Guess the little turd didn't do his homework. The cop came home just as the kid had gained entry, fortunately unarmed.

The intruder was a multi-tasker. He was a burglar but he was also a rapist. After all of the investigation was completed, this nineteen-year-old turned out to have been very busy. They discovered that he had four rapes to his credit.

Who knows how much more he had done?   He is still in Attica. I hope he never gets out. I have no belief that he will ever be anything but what he is right now. But that subject will be for another of our little get-togethers.

Too bad Shaky didn't have to testify! I could just see him sitting on the witness stand, and the lawyer saying, 'Bark, if you see the intruder in the room. And Shakes would bark, then add his now famous, fierce, guttural growl.'

But the swabs did. And that was back when DNA was just taking off.

The Nyack police gave Shaky a little ceremony, his picture was in the Journal News, he got a tiny badge for his collar, a bag of pig's ears and ten pounds of Omaha Steaks. Every steak went to that dog! The kids and I never touched a bite!

I had the house wired up, locked up, window guards put in and the best burglar system I could find, installed. I did the same thing to my new house when I bought it.

The worst thing the little bastard did was destroy my sense of security. And I have thought so much about the women whose lives he destroyed.

I even went through a period where I thought about getting a gun. I went to the range and learned how to shoot. But the more I thought about it, it just was not the solution for me. But I do have a taser gun and pepper spray.

I'll back up a bit and tell you how I got Mr. Tough Guy, Shaky. Lexie is part of this story. I had lost a wonderful Scottie, Mr. McGregor. We called him Max. Another little tough guy. Anyway, I had really been in a mourning period because Max had been my companion during some tough times.

Lexie called me one night about eleven in the evening. At first I was afraid there was a problem because she rarely called that late. I said, 'What's the matter?'

She said, 'Don't get excited, I have a surprise for you.'

My surly side surfaced, and I growled, 'Why would I want a surprise at 11 at night? Are you smoking something?'

Lex laughed and said, 'Hey, make your self somewhat presentable, Hunter and I are coming over.' And she hung up!

I was alternately angry and curious. What could she be bringing over. And she had never come with Hunter without being invited.

In a few minutes, the door bell rang. Lex and Hunter entered and he was carrying the ugliest dog I had ever seen. The dogs paws were tightly wrapped around Hunter's neck. I glared at Lex. 'You better not be thinking that that dog is my surprise. What in God's name is it?'

Hunter laughed, 'Glory Girl, this dog is your personality match. Guess what, he doesn't like strangers. Well, actually, I don't think he likes most people.'

'Well, he seems to like you, you keep him.' I muttered. 'What in the world makes either of you think I want him? He is the ugliest damn dog I have ever seen. If I do get a dog, I want another Scottie. But I don't want another dog. It's the last thing I need. Now take that hideous little tub of a mutt and leave.'

And as I finished saying this, the little, round, bristle-haired mess, walked slowly over to where I was sitting and put his paws on my knees and laid his head in my lap. Sad eyes looking up.

I picked him up and he snuggled right in, his head borrowing into my neck. This was nuts. Hunter had just told me Mr. Ugly did not like people. So why was this dog staking out a claim for my affection?

I said to Hunter, "You have any idea what he is? Does he have a name? How did you get him? And why did you think I would want him?'

Hunter said, 'Slow down, that's a lot of questions. The guys at the station think he might be a dachshund. He might be mixed with something. No name, somebody brought him to the station because he was wandering out on 9W. Amazing that he wasn't hit. And lastly, we think you need each other.'

Well, I have to say that they were right. He was my loving and faithful companion for ten years. Not long after he died, Lex brought me a little, ball of fur that is now sleeping under the covers.

I still have all the burglar alarms and the other stuff, but I know Hamlet is best weapon I have. I will never forget my little hero, my little burglar alarm, Shaky. He still sleeps in my bedroom, in that little brass urn that is on my bedside table.

Mora said, "I would loved to have known Shaky. More guts that most of the men I know."

Mora continued, "I have a doggy tale. This one is about a German Shepherd. Well, two of them actually.

The Drug Dealers Dog

One time when I was about twelve or so, I heard a commotion outside and being a kid, of course I scrambled to go see what was going on. My brothers and I hit the street about the same time.

A car had hit a dog. It was so bad that you couldn't even tell what kind of dog it was. The back leg was shattered and mangled.

My brothers and I got her to the side of the road. By now, a cop came along and assessed the situation and said, "Just let the people come pick up the dog. She needs to be put down."

Of course, since we did not have a clue about how serious it was, we were not going to let that happen.

The boys went and got a board wide enough and long enough that they were able to get her on it and we walked seven blocks to a Vet Hospital. Amazingly, the attendant took one look, and told us to bring her back into the back part of the hospital board and all. They transferred her to a table. The vet and two attendants starting working on her. We were told to go out to the waiting room.

Finally somebody started asking my brother questions about the dog. To everybody's surprise, we told them we did not know who she belonged to. But these wonderful people kept treating her.

Mickey ran home to get Mom. Well, you already know what kind of person she was. She told the vet to do what he had to do and she would have us try to find out who owned the dog, and if we couldn't find the owner, she would pay for everything.

The Dr. looked at my mom and said, 'If it comes to that, all I am going to charge you is for is the medicine. I know how you work with some of the parents who have a hard time paying for childcare at your place.'

Mom nodded gratefully. Then she walked over and hugged the doctor. That was our mom and we were so proud of her.

Dr. Cummings said, 'Go home now. You can come back and visit if you want to, but she is going to be here for a few weeks. I'm pretty sure we can save her but she will have some permanent problems.'

We all walked home arm in arm. Then we started arguing over what we would name her. The names just kept getting weirder and weirder and by the time we got home we were laughing up a storm.

The boys and I went to visit her every day and I know Mom went as much as she could, too. She had done everything to try to find out if the dog had an owner but so far, nothing.

By now, we thought of her as our dog.

We named her Cleo. But Mom made us keep trying to find out if she belonged to anybody. We made posters, put them all over, we knocked on doors and we hoped that nobody would claim her, but we still gave it our best shot.

Cleo was in the hospital for a whole month. But she did get better. She had a stiff leg and a major limp but the rest of her was fine.

Cleo was an incredible dog. Loving, sweet, and fiercely loyal. Almost a year went by and Cleo had become a real part of our family.

One day the door bell rang. I knew not to open the door. We did not open up either at the house or next door at the daycare. I see through the peep that it is a guy that is known in the neighborhood and he is not on anybody's invitation list. So Mickey goes over to get out mother.

The doorstep jerk immediately starts yelling at my mother, that the dog is his and why did we kidnap her? My mother tries to explain and he just kept getting louder and more belligerent.

Mom finally calls the cops. They come, Mom explains, and they ask the guy that if he can prove the dog was his He tells them no, he has no papers. So the cops tell him that Cleo is ours, that too much time has taken place, he can't prove anything and we have been taking care of it and more.

The guy leaves and we think that is the end of it.

It wasn't.

All kinds of stuff starts happening. And he makes threats against us, the daycare, the kids and more.

Finally one day, my mother told us that we had to give the dog back to him. We were all in tears. But Mom was right. We could not take any chances with this jerk. He was dangerous and we were in a very vulnerable situation. We can't jeopardize any of the kids in the daycare. And this nut is very unpredictable and is known to get even with people that he thinks have wronged him.

It was bad for us and it was worse of Cleo.

This was my first experience with how some humans were just pure evil.

One Sunday, a few weeks after we had to give Cleo back to the Monster, as we called him, the vet called Mom. He asked if she would come to his clinic.

So she told me I could come with her, told Mickey to hold down the fort, and we waked over, wondering what he wanted.

He took us back to his office, led us over to a box and lifted out a German Shepherd puppy. Almost pure blonde, huge paws and all soft and snuggly.

Doc said, 'Here, I have a present for you.' Mom asked, 'Why?' I didn't care why, I just reached over and took him out of Doc's arms.

Doc told us that one of his clients, breeders of a champion line of German Shepherds, had a litter and this puppy could not be sold or bred because of his color and he had a birth defect. He was born with his testicles on the inside. They had told him that they were going to give the puppy away and he said that he had the perfect family. He told Mom, the only requirement was that she would have him fixed as soon as he was old enough. My mom said, 'No, problem, you just tell us when.'

My mother embarrassed me by hugging the old vet again and kissing him on both cheeks, but I was very grateful even if I did not show it by doing any hugging, I just nodded, and mumbled thanks and tried to hide my tears.

We took our precious cargo home to show the boys. We had Caesar, (what else would we have named him?) for years. A magnificent dog. He stayed blonde except for a brown saddle and muzzle.

And there is a wonderful, fairytale postscript to the Cleo story. A few months after we got Caesar, the door bell rang, I looked out of the peep hole and there were two cops. I opened the door and they were standing there with Cleo.

The Monster had been killed in some kind of deal-gone-bad and our wonderful neighborhood guys remembered our ordeal with Cleo and they brought her home. We had her for years too. She and Caesar were inseparable. It was almost wall to wall dogs. They used to spend most of their time over at the daycare. Talk about having your own police force. They used to play and interact with the kids. They actually used to play keep-away with the kids. Parents used to even bring the dog toys and treats for both of them.

One time one of the daycare kid's uncle came to pick up his sister's kid and the two dogs got in between him and the boy. My brothers had to take the dogs home so that the uncle could get the kid he came after. We thought it was pretty special of the dogs to be so protective, but I don't think the uncle was too thrilled. He never picked up his nephew again. The kid's mom thought it was hilarious.

I still miss those two gentle giants. They were such a big part of my growing up.

Mora started waving her hands, "Hey, did you think I would not have another story? I know, I am the big mouth, but my Lassies, but, I would prefer to be called The Storyteller, thank you very much! And she laughed that magical throaty laugh of hers.

Glory, you're from New Mexico, I have just been reading about the Storytellers from there. Tonight we have all been Storytellers. The Circle of Life and all that! She laughed at her own silliness, and gushed on, "God, I love this dog topic! This one won't take long."

The Rottweiler Babysitter

Back when I was still working at Sears, I used to work evenings, as I said before. Bill was supposed to be home by six. His only responsibility connected to the family. That would just leave an hour where the kids were by themselves. We had a big Rottweiler. Big teddy bear of a dog. But he was very attached to the kids. But I had never seen a mean side to him. Just a big, slobbering idiot.

One day I called my neighbor, Linda, to check on the kids. She would look outside and tell me if Bill's truck was in the driveway. This particular day she looked out and saw no truck. So I asked her if she would walk over, check on the kids and tell them to call her if they needed anything. About fifteen minutes later, I get a call at work. It's Linda. I say a chirpy 'Hello', she launches right in, 'Mora, in the future, check on your own kids, and you can take that damn dog and stuff him somewhere.'

'What happened?' I ask. Turns out that she had walked over, knocked and opened the door at the same time. She got halfway in and the dog nailed her between the door and the doorframe. And that was not enough for him, he growled deep in his throat and bared his teeth right against her exposed throat.

Fortunately, he let her ease her way back out, continued growling until she was off our property. This produced a very scared Linda who never came back into my house even when I was there.

Mora looked at everybody and said, "OK, I'm ready for another dog story, Who's up?"

JJ looked like she was going to say something, but I cut her off.

People were beginning to come in and our table was needed. I signaled for Pearl to come over to settle us up and we paid our bill, left her a great tip, retrieved our belongings, and marched our way past waiting patrons who were there for a late lunch.

We ambled out to the big boat of a car and climbed in for our short jaunt back to my house.

"What is your pleasure Ladies," and before I could continue five voices said, "Go Home", and Lex who had her head on my shoulder and was idly fingering my ring, said, "Yeah, Sweet Cheeks, I think we are all exhausted. But I want to say something to everybody. This party has been so wonderful for so many reasons. I know you all love me and I love you."

Mora chirped in, "Lexie girl, this has been a great big group therapy session. We all feel better. And yes, Birthday Girl, we love you. And you can take that to the bank!"

"What the big deal is, that for the very first time in my life, I have spent the last several months feeling sorry for myself. I've even tried to hide it from Glory. I put on my happy face and keep moving. And this past week it all just came to a explosion point."

"Tonight has knocked that all out. All of the stories have made me see that we all deal with issues, other people's failures and just life. Life *is* messy. But mostly life is good. And I guess I have to admit that a lot of it is great."

I squeezed her hand in support.

Lex continued, "I have known Viv for a long time. I never told Glory, but I was always so envious of her perfect life. Sometimes I even resented it. But the fact is that none of us every really know about what another person has to endure. We rarely know what is really inside. So I need to remember to appreciate what is good. And work on making what isn't , better. I have always prided myself on not being judgmental. But the truth is that we all make judgments and so often with out all of the facts. I am going to try to be better at not being such a know-it-all."

"I know I sound all goody-goody schmaltzy but I really do mean it."

Everybody in the car was nodding and murmuring in agreement.

Everyone was very quiet until we reached my house. We all piled out.

We stood in the driveway, and JJ starting singing Happy Birthday to Lex. We joined in with a very loud and lusty, two choruses.

Everybody dashed inside, used bathrooms, gathered belongings and one at a time, said another happy birthday, more goodbyes with much hugging and the house emptied except for Lex and me.

She started to say something and I grabbed her in a bear hug and said, "Lex, I know."

She gave me a long look and grinned and said, "Well, Damn, Girl, you know what Scarlet said, 'I can't think about it now, after all, tomorrow is another day! I'll think about it later.'

And she scooted out the door.

I looked at Hamlet who had come out of hiding underneath the covers, his refuge when the house was filled with loud womenfolk.

"Well, my fine, four-footed friend, what do you think about all of this? I sat down on the chaise and he snuggled happily into my lap.

Lex was right. Things are good. I was still grieving about Viv and I would continue to grieve up to the day I died. There could be no doubt about that. But I still had a job to do.

I would continue to try to be there for Viv's children for as long as I was breathing. I was not a substitute mother, but I could be an aunt who was there for them and hopefully someday, for Viv's grandchildren.

Damon has become a more hands-on father. Viv would be very proud of him.

The circle of life does go on.

It occurred to me that I was happy. Happiness had snuck up on me and settled in without my paying much attention.

I had a great job. Didn't make much money but boy did it pay off when I saw my little ducklings go out and change the world.

I had four wonderful children who were changing the world themselves. There were some problems with the older ones, but we would get past that. We always did.

Viv's children and future grandchildren would be a part of that continuing circle of life.

Hamlet scooched around and raised his body until he could put his head on my shoulder and gave a great, contented sigh.

I sighed too. You can't keep a good woman down. And you certainly can't keep the six of us down.

The fact is that I really have two families. Love has built both. I wondered what would be next for all of us. Life does have a way of moving on.

I was surprised that I was not tired or sleepy. Our night of The Storytellers had not enervated me, it had done just the opposite. I was jazzed, as the kids say. Ready for whatever life was going to throw it me. My turn at bat.

2:33 PM

Just then the phone rang. It was Mia. "Mom, where are you? Why are you still home? You were supposed to be here by lunch. You know the family is waiting for you to get here."

"I'm on my way, Honey. I'm on my way."

Judianne Lee is a retired school teacher. She taught Language Arts in St. David, AZ

She was a National speaker for Fire Science and Fire Safety and developed Train-the-Trainer programs for fire departments as well as the development of fire science and fire safety materials.

ESL and English for Cochise College

English for Paradise Valley Community College

English for Shadow Mt. High School

English for Vista Verde Middle School

Ms. Lee Moved to Richardson, TX in 2008

She lives with her three canine companions, Lexie, Lucy and Odie and is currently working on her next novel, *BEFORE I DIE.*

Read an excerpt from *Roxie's Angels*

by Judianne Lee

Available from Lulu.com and Amazon.com

Also available for downloading and eBook

ROXIE'S ANGELS

Aug 1

El Con is not acting like himself.   He seems to have no energy and now it is very clear that he is favoring that leg.

Aug 2

Been in the barn with El.   Doc has been coming and going.   He has diagnosed El's problem as laminitis.   Now El is shifting his weight off his front legs and extending them.

I had heard about laminitis but I really did not know much about it.   So Doc gave me a pretty quick crash course.   Turns out this is pretty nasty stuff.   I actually had to write down what he said because most of the terms that he used were new to me.

Doc said that laminitis is a vascular disease that goes with ischemia or homeostasis and has to do with the laminae of the hoof.   This laminae is what secures the coffin bone to the hoof wall.   If it gets inflamed and cannot be fixed, the coffin bone could become detached from the horny wall.   It could sink or "founder".

This will sound really silly of me, but I have just never thought of El Con being sick.   He has been one of those outrageously healthy beasts and has never had any of the normal problems even.   I am scared out of my mind.   But Doc said that because he has such a strong constitution he should be able to be treated successfully.

So please, let this be true.   I just can't handle being without him. He is so much a part of me and what keeps me grounded and gives me solace and I guess I could go on forever about that but for now if will just use all the resources for "making things better" that I can think of.

Joe helped me make a bed with two bedrolls and he scrounged up three pillows. Brownie sent down some clean blankets so I am all set. It should only be for a couple of more days anyway.

Aug 3

Sometime during the night El woke me up by going down in a thump. It was as if he just felt that his legs could no longer hold him up. And when I felt him, he had a fever. The hoof had been very hot last night and Doc F. said that was from the infection.

Now I see this is beyond what I had hoped would be the outcome. He has really gotten much worse is such a short space of time.   Doc said he is doing everything he can.   I believe him. Unfortunately I am questioning everything else in life.   Right now I would bargain to be the best, most perfect person just to put this right.

Aug 4

Doc F. was here just after 6 AM. Thank goodness. He has started El on some very strong medicine mix to control the fever.

Dad was questioning how this could happen so fast and what could have caused it. Doc said that it can even be caused by a difference in diet and that El may have found something different that he had eaten when he was out of the barn and by himself.

Dad had brought out doughnuts, biscuits and sausage and strawberries in cream. I know he is trying so hard to help.

"Rox, Honey bun, you have to eat. It is not going to help El if you make yourself sick. If you are going to stay out here I have to know that you are eating."

And he kept talking about the coming school year and other stuff but I finally said, "Dad, I don't want to talk." Just let me spend this time with him. He gave me a long, sad look, "I will be up at the house with Brownie."

He had barely left and Joe came into the stall. El did not move but just watched me with a look that clearly said he did not understand why this was happening to him. I have never felt so helpless. To love a creature so much who has loved you and yet not be able to take away the pain to explain why, and worse, to know the inevitable. I have been around these animals too long not to know.

Joe sat down by me on the bedroll. "Roxie Girl, you need to get away for a few minutes. You have not left here for three days. You are even using the barn outhouse and we all know how you feel about that. Go up to the house and get a shower. You look horrible and you don't smell much better. Go take a walk, or better yet, take Topper out and get a quick ride. I promise I will stay until you get back."

I shook my head, talking just seemed to take too much effort. I gave him a light punch on his arm and he surprised my by grabbing me and giving me a big bear hug.

"OK, but let me go get you some clean clothes. How about I make you a soda bucket? I will get a block of ice in town when I go get you some clothes. I'll call Gretchen and she can get you some clean levis and a shirt."

Joe got up and in minutes, Wade came in. It was turning into a parade.

"Gosh, Wade, it is your turn to babysit?"

Wade did not do a very good job of acting innocent. "Nah, I'm just using this for an excuse to get off ole' June Bug. I been ridin' fence for three days and my back side's askin' my legs to do some work.

"Oh, Wade, I'm so sorry, you are doing my job!"

Rox, my girl, I ain't complainin'. We all do what needs doin'. I just want to know you are you are both getting' on OK. Listen, my Junie got lame, you 'member? Everybody thought she was a goner. She went down, stayed down two days and alls the sudden, she stands up and she come back and now she nigh perfect. With horses, you never know what's going to happen. With cow's its different. Cow goes down, its done for. But I seen horses get right fixed just one step away from the glue factory. Oh, Honey, I'm sorry, I shouldn't say that. But you know what I mean."

"Wade, I know. And I appreciate how much you all care. Now go tell the rest of the guys, I am fine. I'll yell if I am not.

Now Wade reached over and gave me a very quick hug. Boy, talk about mixed emotions, I loved that they cared so much, but their concern also told me that I was right that things were bad and getting worse.

Both El and I slept fitfully for a couple of hours. I woke up each time he had tried to move. I could feel him trying to make his body do what he wanted it to do. He couldn't.

Joe came back with my clothes, a bucket full of chopped ice and Cokes and Nehi orange sodas. He had a bag with two hamburgers and a mountain of fries. We had a nice lunch sitting side by side on little bed/couch. After we ate, Joe and I just sat there, I leaned my head on his shoulder and we did not talk, he just let me stay quiet and I knew both of us were remembering all the times with El over the years. Finally, I told him that I was fine, I knew he had stuff to do.

"Roxie, girl, tell me what you need before I get back to work."

I asked him to go get me two buckets of clean water, a bar of soap, and a couple towels.

When he brought them back I asked him to stand "guard" while I cleaned up. He went out and I cleaned up as well as I could, then put on the clean clothes. Then I stretched out by El and we took another short nap.

I pushed my makeshift bed over to El and I have spent the rest day laying next to him with my body stretched out along his back. James came out and we have taken turns trying to cool him down with wet cloths. But his temp has just climbed.

James went inside and talked to Dad who had not left Brownie's all day. He asked Dad if it was OK if he stayed in the Barn. Dad said he thought it was a good idea.

The vet came back out and said things were not getting better. Dad and Brownie came out and now we were all taking turns keeping El cool and trying to make him comfortable. Horrible sounds were coming from him and long deep shudders.

I wanted to stay tight against him but was afraid of making him too hot so I laid as close as I could and I know that he could feel that it was my touch. I kept rubbing his neck in that special sweet spot that he always liked.

I just could not sleep. Joe had put bed rolls in the next stall. Dad and Brownie had put up a makeshift table out of saw horses and boards and cook kept it loaded up and with food. Cook kept bringing out hot coffee and more food.

If the situation had not been so serious it would have been a perfect party. Good friends together, sharing food, stories and concern for each other. They all love both El Con and me. I felt so much love for them and love for El and fear for what could happen. I was just overwhelmed with emotion. I was afraid if I talked I would start crying and not be able to stop.

The hands were dropping by and checking in and sitting with us in what had now become a "waiting room" stall.

Eventually Dad fell asleep, Brownie went back up to the house. James bunked down on his bedroll a couple of feet away from my goofy bed and he would reach over and pat my hand every so often. He drifted off to sleep and I think El and I slept a patchy sleep. Every sound and move he made woke me up.

At 2:16 in the morning, El's breathing became "different". He was making such an effort. I wrapped my self as tightly to him as I could and told he did not have to fight anymore. He had fought like the warrior that he was. He sighed, and shuddered and life left his magnificent body. I could not move. I laid there until the sun was just coming up before I called out to dad to tell him that it was over.

Both Dad and James got up. Dad said, "When did it happen?" I told him and he said, "OK, James, you go on home. She will call you later." I nodded. He held my hand for a minute, kissed me on the top of my head, and he walked slowly out of the barn.

Dad gently pulled me to my feet. "Roxie, you have to go inside. You have done everything you could. Now you have to let me take care of the rest of it. Brownie and I have been talking and we want you to look at a place for him but not until tomorrow. I am going to take care of everything out here. Joe, Wade and I are going to do it right. You don't have to worry."

Just then Joe came in and pulled me out of the barn and walked with me up to the house. Brownie met us at the door. He told Joe to take me into the front bedroom that was faced away from the barn. I didn't understand why I had not cried yet. I just felt hollow. I could not breathe and my head was splitting open.

Brownie's cook brought me a bowl of ice and she was soaking wash cloths in the ice water and telling me to put it on my face. Suddenly the door to the room opened and Doc Harlan was there.

"OK, girl who thinks she is Wonder Woman, I am going to help. He gave me a shot of something, and the rest of the day was a merciful blur.

And the next was almost the same. I slept for most of it. In the middle of the next night, I got up and went out to the barn. I don't know why, but it was almost to the minute when I had lost him.

I stood in the stall and now the tears came. Floods. I couldn't stop, I couldn't breathe, and then I was screaming. Joe got there first, then Wade, some of the other hands, and then there was Dad, Brownie and even Brownie's cook. Joe looked ashen. The rest did not look much better. Dad kept saying "It's OK, It's OK, Don't Cry." Joe pushed Dad away and spoke in a quiet but very firm voice, "Harrison, leave her alone. She needs this. Better this than keeping it all in." I sank down to El's spot. I could still smell his wonderful clean horse smell. Joe brought me his bridle and put it in my hands.

He said firmly, OK, let's all go outside. She is fine in here. And they all left. I don't know how long I stayed. Finally, still clutching his bridle, I walked out, Joe was leaned against the fence and he walked me back up to the house and did not say a word. Wonderful, understanding Joe. Always knowing just what I need.

Dad asked if I wanted to go home or stay at Brownies. I said "Let's go home."

James called daily. We chatted briefly but he got that I was not ready to see him or anybody else.

I never knew there could be grief like this. I alternated between gut deep pain and feeling as if there was a huge hollow hole in my chest and wanting to run screaming. But I did not know where I could run to. For so many of my growing up years, when I had a problem or was hurting or sad, I had been able to go to El Con, saddle up and he would put me back together piece by piece.

Who was going to put me back together now? I had thought I had been hurt by Ida with the name calling and what she had done when she hurt me or destroyed what belonged to me. Now I knew that was nothing. Nothing! This hurt did not go away. It just seemed to keep burning bigger.

I was not able to go with Dad and Brownie to pick out the place for him. I knew the place they were talking about and it would be fine. So they made all the plans and they buried him. It was nine days before I could go out to his resting place.

It is the highest spot on Brownie's ranch. It is a small mesa ridge but there must be some underground water because of the trees. It has lush walnut and fragrant peach trees. So there is shade. Joe and Wade had made a beautiful mesquite bench. Somebody had gone to Tucson and gotten grass. The kind that comes in squares and you put over dirt and it makes a beautiful, instant green lawn. And flowers. This will be a wonderful, peaceful place to come to visit him. Wade does great carvings and he has already started one of El Conquistador.

I know gut deep that this is a grief that will never leave me. Joe says that I have to turn all of these memories to positive ones. I have the feeling that he has had his own "griefs" and he has learned to do this. For the first time I also have a deeper understanding about the way that Dad feels about Ida. No matter what she has done or what has happened he really loves her. I hope that will make it easier for me to understand why he kept bringing her back home. I get that he is having such a hard time living without her. And he made the supreme sacrifice to have two homes to keep us separated most of the time.

Dad had gotten my Angel Crew together. Even Mary Jane and her mother. Everyone was there. A real funeral for El Con. I know it was for both of us. I carried his bridle that I had intertwined with white roses and babies breath. And Joe had left a little open hole that I put three of his favorite stall toys into. I sang an Irish lullaby to him, _Toura Lura,_ all of my wonderful people, joined in on the second chorus. He had always let me know he loved it when I sang to him and I know that somewhere he hears. Now there is another angle watching out for me.

I pulled the flowers off of the bridle and laid them on the grassy plot. His bridle will hang on my mirror so I see it every day before I even see me. His show bridle. His every day bridle is going to hang in the living room over the fireplace. Dad is going to ask Ted to do a portrait of El. But he might not. I know he has been asked before and has refused. But he knows other artists and we can get one of them to paint the portrait.

Everybody left except for James. We sat on El Con's bench until sunset. Not talking. Just there. It was mid-August but there had been enough rain to keep down the worst of the heat. I don't think we really paid attention anyway.

As we walked back down what was now called El Con's Mesa, James asked me if I would let him make a wood and silver plaque for his resting place.   I told him I thought that was a thoughtful, tender idea.